DENNIS
in JURASSIC BARK

Studio Press
An imprint of Bonnier Books UK
The Plaza, 535 King's Road,
London, SW10 0SZ

www.studiopressbooks.co.uk

www.beano.com

A Beano Studios Product © D.C. Thomson Ltd 2019

Written and illustrated by Nigel Auchterlounie

A CIP catalogue record for this book
is available from the British Library.

Paperback: 978-1-78741-279-8

Printed and bound by Clays Ltd, Elcograf S.p.A

2 4 6 8 10 9 7 5 3 1

Studio Press is an imprint of Bonnier Books UK
www.bonnierbooks.co.uk

AN EPIC BEANO® ADVENTURE

DENNIS
in JURASSIC BARK

STUDIO PRESS

A WORD FROM THE AUTHOR

It had been a year since I'd written my bestselling (for 23 minutes) book *Dennis and the Chamber of Mischief*, and my publisher was shouting at me to write another one.

Actually sitting next to me, in the coffee shop, shouting at me.

"WRITE! GO ON, WRITE! WRITE A BOOK! DO IT!" she screamed through the megaphone that was pressed against my ear. Writers love to write (or pretend to write) in coffee shops. So everyone knows how clever they are.

My publisher wanted an idea at least as amazing as the last

4

story. Something that would be a bestseller for 24 minutes, maybe even 25. But I couldn't think of one!

You see, I didn't think of the last one. The last story had been told to me by a kid called Dennis. You may have heard of him.

My publisher looked at her watch. "Right! I've got to go. I've got to make two poets cry before lunch." She smiled warmly, then slapped the keyboard. **"WRITE!"** she repeated, before swishing out.

What was I meant to do? Feeling hopeless, I looked around the coffee shop for inspiration. The guy behind the counter who'd served me my coffee was huge with an equally huge beard. He was obviously going for the hipster look but had ended up looking more like a Viking. The horned helmet he was wearing didn't help. Would my publisher accept a story about a hipster Viking?

DING! The shop bell rang as someone entered – well, sneaked in. It was Dennis.

DENNIS! I thought loudly to myself. Perfect! I need that kid to tell me another exciting story.

Just then, an elephant crept in after him.

I'm no expert, but I know an elephant when I see one. Even if the elephant is wearing a hat, a trench coat and dark glasses.

"Excuse me," said Dennis, as he and the elephant squeezed past a table stacked high with

coffee cups. The writer at that table was looking nearly as desperate as I had been feeling a few minutes ago. The writer let out a wail and continued with their not-writing.

CRASH! went the table and everything on it, as the elephant's enormous butt knocked it over.

"Excuse me," said Dennis, as he and the elephant squeezed past yet another writer.

CRASH!! went the table and everything on it, as the elephant's enormous butt knocked that over too, spilling coffee all over the writer's laptop.

"Excuse me," said Dennis.

CRASH!!!

"Excuse me," said Dennis.

CRASH! CRASH!

Elephants are bad at sneaking past things.

Finally, Dennis and the poorly disguised elephant reached the back of the coffee shop and sat down, leaving the angry writers to wipe their laptops and glare angrily in their direction. The elephant picked up a copy of the *Beanotown Gazette* and pretended to read it. The headline, in huge letters on the front page, read:

ESCAPED ELEPHANT STILL AT LARGE!

I quickly shut my laptop and zigzagged around the fallen tables.

At the back of the shop, I sat down at the same table as Dennis and the poorly disguised elephant.

Dennis gave me one of his grumpy "What do you want?!" looks, then said, "What do you want?!"

"Another story," I answered simply.

"I haven't got any other stories," he replied.

"You're sitting next to an escaped zoo elephant," I pointed out.

"Hey – I have no idea who this gentleman is!" Dennis protested. "We just arrived at the same time, that's all. He doesn't look like an elephant to me. If I had to make a guess, I'd say he was a French spy."

I pulled my phone out. "So you won't be bothered if I call the zoo?" I asked.

Dennis grabbed my phone and plonked it into a cup of cold tea that someone had left behind. "What do you want to know?"

"Tell me about another one of your adventures," I said.

Dennis scowled at me, then told me the story of what's hidden on Duck Island...

THE BIT BEFORE THE OPENING CREDITS

Eeny, meeny, miny, moe, thought the huge asteroid, as it floated through space 65 million years ago. Which planet shall I crash into?...

(Okay, some of you might have read the first book and just realised that same "Eeny, meeny" bit was near the start. I'm not just copying huge chunks of the last book to fatten out this one... Okay, maybe I am, but there's also a second reason – it's got something to do with this story too. You'll see.)

...That's always a tricky question for an asteroid to answer.

It had gone past a tiny one, which wasn't much of a planet at all. Then a blue one. Then a nice, rocky, red one the asteroid thought it could leave a lovely crater in. (Asteroids love to leave craters in things). But then it spotted a cheeky blue and green planet and immediately disliked it. It seemed to be saying, "Aren't I awesome? I've got a breathable atmosphere! I've got life on me. Look!" Just like that kid at school who gets better birthday presents than you.

So Dennis the asteroid crashed into Earth and killed all the dinosaurs.

Did I mention the asteroid was called Dennis? Well, it was. How do I know? I named it!

Dennis the asteroid crashed into the bit of Earth that would become Beanotown 65 million years later. It burnt through the atmosphere, heating up to a million degrees and bursting into some really quite satisfying flames, before smashing into the planet with enough force to rip open time itself.

The explosion threw enough dust into the atmosphere to black out the sun for years, resulting in a 10-year-long winter that killed all but a few of the dinosaurs.

The explosion had also ripped open a hole in time and

*blown a sort of giant bubble that bounced forwards,
into the future. Fifty-nine dinosaurs of various types
were caught up in it. Whoa! they thought. We're
caught up in a floaty time bubble! We sure hope it
drops us off somewhere safe.*

*Eventually, the time bubble full of dinosaurs
came to rest, 11 years after Dennis the asteroid hit.
Just as the sun was beginning to shine again.*

The descendants of these dinosaurs still live

in Beanotown now – on Duck Island, in the middle of the park.

I know what you're thinking... 65 million years is a bit far back to begin a story about a 10-year-old boy. It takes starting at the beginning to a whole new level – but stick with me...

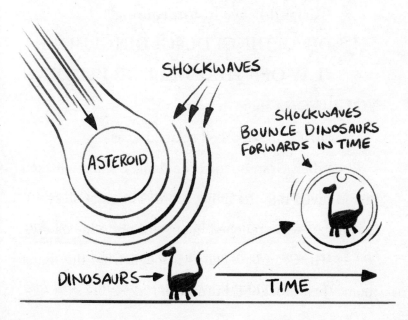

THE ACTUAL START OF THE ACTUAL STORY

DING! DING! DING! DING! DING! DING!

The DONG on Gran's doorbell had stopped working months ago.

DING! DING! DING! DING!

"I'm coming!" Gran shouted, as she headed for the front door.

DING! DING! DING! DING!

"Alright! Leave it! I'm coming!"

DING! DING! DING! DING! DING!

"LAY OFF THAT BELL OR I'LL DING YOU!!!" Gran shouted.

DING? the doorbell seemed to ask.

When Gran opened the door, Dennis whisked in and dived into the living room. The right sleeve of his jumper was drenched in custard up to the elbow.

"Hi, Gran," he called through from the living room. "Just thought I'd drop by."

Dennis's dog Gnasher calmly strolled inside, leaving custardy paw prints on the carpet. He gave Gran his best "Don't ask" look. She sighed and shut the door.

A few minutes later, Gran entered the living room with a cup of tea, a carton of juice and the biscuit tin.

Dennis was slouched down low on the couch. Super slouchy low. It was his best I-don't-want-anyone-to-see-the-back-of-my-head-from-the-window slouch.

Gran smiled. "What have you done now, Dennis?" she asked.

"Hey! What happened to innocent until proven guilty?" Dennis protested, guiltily.

"Have it your way." Gran turned on the telly.

It was Beanotown local news, and the newsreader was just finishing a report.

"... leaving the high street covered in custard."

The newsreader was handed a piece of paper from off-screen.

"And now, we have a late breaking-news story. Over to our reporter on the scene for more."

The picture changed to the station's roving reporter.

"Thank you, John," the reporter started. "I'm reporting to you live from Beanotown Beach, where what seems to be a huge mutant seagull is stealing ice creams from anyone who buys one from Mr Icy!"

The camera spun round to show the huge, flapping beast stealing the ice creams.

"Arrrgh!" Mr Icy screamed from his van. "It's after this new trout-flavoured ice cream!" He threw a big tub of grey, fishy-looking ice cream out of the window and slid it firmly shut.

Dennis sat forward.

That was no mutant seagull. It was a

Pterodactyl! (Which is apparently spelt with a P, even though you don't say it. What's that all about?)

"Fake news!" Gran announced. "That'll be CGI, I bet you!"

As they watched, the Pterodactyl greedily gobbled up the gross-looking ice cream.

Dennis knew his CGI. He could spot it a mile away.

"That's real, Gran," he told her. "That's a Pterodactyl! I should know."

If there was one thing Dennis was an expert on – and there was only one thing – it was dinosaurs. (Oh and catapults... and skateboarding. Okay, that's three things. But he knew a lot about dinos.)

Dinosaur? thought Gran, and she opened her mouth to say something surprising and extremely interesting...

OTHER, OTHER EYES

Across town, a custard-covered Walter staggered into his home.

He was furious with Dennis. All he'd tried to do was utterly destroy Dennis's skateboard. There was no need to do that thing with the fire engine full of custard!

Walter stormed into the utility room (a room that posh people have for washing machines and dryers) and peeled off his custard-soaked clothes. He could hear the local news blaring on the kitchen TV.

He was furious with Dennis's dog too. Just as Walter had managed to dodge the custardy flood, Gnasher had done one of his gnashy barks, making Walter stumble back... into the custard torrent.

Thinking back, Walter could remember plenty of times when one evil scheme or another of his would have worked against Dennis, if it weren't for that awful dog of his jumping in at the last minute.

As he tiptoed past the kitchen TV in his underpants and vest, Walter saw that the news report was coming from Beanotown Beach.

"... where what seems to be a huge mutant seagull is stealing ice creams from anyone who buys one from Mr Icy!"

Walter also knew his dinosaurs. That was no mutant seagull. He stared in admiration – yellow, soggy and custardy.

Walter needed something to even things up between him and Dennis. Something that would go past making things even, and go really quite far into things being unfairly stacked on Walter's side.

A Pterodactyl would do that!

"That's my new pet," he said to himself.

Meanwhile, not far away, other eyes were watching the same thing on a completely different telly. And those eyes belonged to Minnie the Minx.

And she was thinking, I wonder if you need stirrups to ride a mutant seagull?

Across town, school pupil Helen was feeling nervous. She was on her first day of work experience.

The school had placed her friend Zoe at the swimming pool. From what Zoe said, it was pretty easy work but a bit boring. Helen, however, had been sent to work with the Mayor of Beanotown.

The work there was pretty easy too – mostly making cups of tea – but there was also a worrying evilness behind everything. For example, as she carried a tray of tea and biscuits through to the Mayor's office, Helen found Mayor Wilbur Brown rubbing his hands together and grinning at his computer screen.

"I'm thinking about money, Helen," the Mayor told her. Chuckling evilly. He seemed to be watching a dinosaur movie on his wall screen. "What could you do with such a formidable creature?"

MUTANT SEAGULL ATTAC[K]

What Helen didn't know was that Wilbur had recently bought a controlling share in Beanotown's zoo. It was pretty run down, and somehow the elephant kept escaping. A new attraction would bring in the money needed to spruce the place up. A dragon would bring in money, and may come in handy with controlling the people of Beanotown.

Then he wondered if it breathed fire. That would be useful.

"Tea?" asked Helen.

Wilbur grabbed the mug, waved her out of his office and dialled Beanotown police station.

"Hello? Beanotown police station and chip shop," answered Chief O'Reilly.

"Chip shop?" the Mayor asked. "What do you mean 'chip shop'?"

"Is that yourself, Mayor Wilbur?" the Chief asked. "Just a joke, sir, ahem..."

The Mayor sighed and started to explain about the dragon, but was interrupted by another voice in the background.

"Cod bites, large chips and mushy peas with curry sauce. Swimming in vinegar please, Chief.

Oh, and stick a battered sausage on that an' all, will you?"

The Mayor frowned while Chief O'Reilly laughed nervously over the phone. "I'll be getting you no such thing, person I don't know! This is a police station. Be gone with ya!"

The Mayor rolled his eyes and shouted down the phone, **"JUST GET DOWN TO THE BEACH AND ARREST THAT DRAGON!!!"**

And with that, he slammed the phone down.

At the police station/chip shop, Chief O'Reilly thought,

DRAGON?

HOW MANY FOURS ARE IN TWENTY-THREE?

"That dinosaur has probably come from Duck Island," said Gran.

Dennis was surprised and extremely interested. "You know about Duck Island?"

Gran was equally shocked. "*You* know about Duck Island?"

Dennis dipped a custard cream into his custard-soaked right sleeve, to make it extra custardy. Then, before jamming it in his mouth, he grabbed a nearby lamp and shone it in Gran's face, interrogation style. "Tell me what you know about Duck Island!" he shouted.

Gran calmly turned the lamp off and said, "Well..."

Dennis heard a strange twinkly music, and everything started to go a bit wibbly wobbly.

"Woah!" shouted Dennis. "What's happening?"

"It feels like a flashback to me," Gran said, taking an old photo album out of the sideboard.

"You know how I feel about flashbacks!" said Dennis.

Gnasher, who was trying to sleep, opened one eye. Gran and Dennis were being quite inconsiderate.

"It's flashback or nothing, I'm afraid! If I flick through these photos while I talk, it should help speed things up."

She opened the big leather bound book.

"Well..." said Gran, as the strange twinkly music started again and everything started to go a bit wibbly wobbly...

Seventy years ago, when Gran was 10, Gran wasn't called Gran. She was called Catherine. Katie, for short. And 70 years ago, Katie was bored.

She sat with the same menace scowl that Dennis thought he'd invented, and shouted, "I'm bored!"

"Catherine Menace," Mr Teacherson said.

"This is History! It's not meant to be 'fun' or 'exciting'. It's meant to be history!"

Then he went back to arguing with the guy who rented the boats on the duck pond in Beanotown park.

"Is there no discount for numbers? Rent two boats get a third free?" he asked.

The boat rental guy looked like the most bored man alive. Mr Teacherson looked at the class gathered by the water's edge.

"I think we can all fit into two boats!"

"No you won't." The boat rental guy yawned. "It's four to a boat, max. To get yourself and all these kids over to the island you'll need... er..."

"Go on," Mr Teacherson said. "How many? There are 22 pupils here. Twenty-three if you include me. Four people to a boat. How many times does four go into 23? With how many left over?"

He turned to the scattered class.

"Children, pay attention! This is an example of how you'll need maths when you grow up."

"I don't need to know how many fours go into 23!" Boat Rental Guy shouted at Mr Teacherson. "I just need to know not to let five into a boat!"

Mr Teacherson had had enough. Which wasn't unusual. **"Everybody back on the bus!"** he shouted.

Once everyone was back on board, Mr Teacherson threw the bus into gear, stamped on the accelerator and the bus lurched forward, towards the duck pond.

He's not going to... boat rental guy began to wonder, but he didn't get to finish his thought before the school bus plunged into the water.

THE FATHER OF ICARUS

School buses don't float.

School buses sink.

But it was only a duck pond, so it was only three feet deep.

Water poured into the bus through the thousands of little holes and gaps that old buses have, and quickly covered the floor.

Catherine Menace lifted her feet, so as not to get them wet, as Mr Teacherson crunched into another gear. Katie and the other kids climbed up onto the seats as the water got deeper.

"Urrrgh, sir! Me butt's wet!" shouted Petey Sweety.

"Pipe down back there!" Mr Teacherson shouted over his shoulder.

"You should have gone before we set off!" Judy Soon teased.

"I've not wet meself!" Petey protested.

"The bus is full of duck water!"

The bus was now well past halfway to the island, and was bumping and struggling up out of the water.

Finally the bus climbed up out of the water and crashed through the bushes into, and onto, Duck Island.

Extricating a small weed from his hair, Mr

Teacherson started his tour lecture. "As you can see, children, Duck Island appears bigger on the inside than the outside."

Mr Teacherson was right. From the park, the island in the middle of the duck pond looked to be about the size of a house – but now they were on it, the island was huge.

"This is because everything on Duck Island is tiny, shrunk down to a fraction of its normal size," Mr Teacherson continued.

"Nothing's small here, sir!" Jerry Jakes pointed out. "Look! It's all big!" Jerry waved his hands about at the surrounding bigness.

"Everything appears to be big because we are also shrunk to a fraction of our normal size," Mr Teacherson explained.

"Eh? When did that happen?" Katie Menace asked.

"If I were small," Jerry said, "I'd be able to fit in my bag, but I can't!"

"That's because your bag has shrunk too!" Mr Teacherson explained loudly, over his shoulder.

"How come I can still reach the luggage rack, if I'm tiny?" asked Brenda Blort.

"Because the bus has shrunk too!!!" Mr Teacherson shouted. "Everything's shrunk! It all shrunk at the same time. You, me, your bags, the bus, your sandwiches – everything's shrunk!"

"My sandwiches haven't shrunk," said Jeremy Sedentary.

"YES, THEY HAVE!!" Mr Teacherson screamed. "Everything has shrunk!"

"No, they haven't. I left them at home," Jeremy informed him.

"QUIET!" Mr Teacherson barked. He cleared his throat and gestured out of the window to his left. "If you look to your left, you'll see an Apatosaurus, one of the sauropod family."

Everyone looked out of the left side of the bus (apart from Brenda, who looked out of the right,

32

because she was still a bit woolly on left and right).

"Sauropods are the long-necked dinosaurs," Jerry informed his classmates. Everyone rolled their eyes.

"How were we shrunk?" Katie Menace asked.

"Oh. It's, like, some sort of gravity-squashy thingy from a do-hicky in the middle of the island. It squashes stuff small," Mr Teacherson replied.

"He never said that!" Dennis exclaimed, interrupting the flashback.

"Woah! Hey, what are you doing?" asked Gran. "You're spoiling the flashback."

"Yeah, but teachers don't talk like that. You were making it up!"

"Okay, okay," Gran admitted. "He started talking science stuff about gravity and squashing, and I didn't really listen."

She was cradling the photo album on her lap, and one of the pictures caught Dennis's eye.

"Who's that?" he asked, pointing at a statue of

a bearded guy in a towel and what looked like fake wings on his back.

"That's Daedalus, the father of Icarus," Gran said.

"Who?"

"It's from Greek mythology. Daedalus built the Labyrinth to keep the Minotaur in," Gran told Dennis.

"Never heard of him," Dennis said.

"What do they teach you in school, these days?" Gran asked.

"How should I know?!" said Dennis. "Anyway, get back to the thing."

"Thing?"

"The reason all that stuff fits on Duck Island. How does it get shrunk?"

"I don't know!" exclaimed Gran. "It sounded like a dumb sci-fi thing... like a compression field." She paused. "That's it!"

"What's it?" asked Dennis.

"The thing that squashes everything down small is called a compression field."

HOW TO TELL LEFT FROM RIGHT

Foreshadowing is this clever thing that clever writers do where something is mentioned in a story and it doesn't seem all that important at the time but ends up being a big deal later. My publisher wants me to put some in, so keep your clever little eyes peeled, reader...

"How were we shrunk?" Katie Menace asked.

"By a compression field that comes from the centre of the island," Mr Teacherson said. "The asteroid that hit here 65 million years ago was... is... a superheavy object. Superdense. It has so much gravity that it squashes everything near it to a fraction of its size."

Petey yawned. "I thought this was History? That sounds more like science."

"If anything were to happen to the asteroid at the centre of the island," Mr Teacherson explained to the class, "the compression field could fail. If that happened, all the dinosaurs on the island would grow back to their normal size and spread out across Beanotown."

Petey rolled his eyes. "Now it sounds like foreshadowing!"

Mr Teacherson ignored Petey and gestured towards the windscreen. "If you look ahead, you'll see a, er... Condorraptor?"

He was guessing a little bit. The creature on the path in front of the bus was the same height as a person, if that person was five foot eight, but more than twice that in length.

"Spinosaurus!" Brenda shouted.

"No. It's not a Spino," Mr Teacherson said. "A Spinosaurus is much, much bigger, with a long crocodile-like snout and a tall sail along the back."

"No!" Brenda shouted. "A Spinosaurus, there on the left! Look!"

Everyone looked out of the left side of the bus.

There was nothing there. The children scoured the dense foliage for a Spinosaurus, but couldn't spot anything like that.

Katie scowled, "There's nothing—" Then stopped mid-sentence. Through the undergrowth, in the shadows... was that a Viking?

Suddenly, from the right, a huge Spinosaurus clamped its enormous jaws down onto the bus. **CRUNCH!**

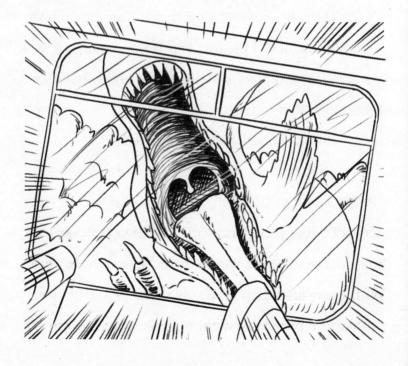

"Brenda, you're 10!" Mr Teacherson shouted. "You should know left from right by now!"

(Personally, I'm on Brenda's side. I always had trouble with left and right. I didn't figure it out until I was 32, but if you hold your hands out like this, the thumb and forefinger on your left hand make an L. That's how I remember now.)

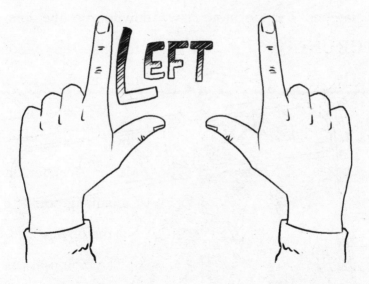

The Spinosaurus probably thought the school bus was some sort of juicy, bus-sized herbivore. With a powerful grip on the roof, the fantastic beast pushed the bus away with its foot, hoping to rip off some juicy meat. This being a bus, though, there was just metal and glass.

The bus slipped from the Spinosaurus's grip and tipped onto its side. Everyone inside fell over, and this tipped the bus over onto its roof, then onto

its other side as it picked up speed. Inside, everyone felt like they were in a tumble dryer.

"We're rolling down a hill!" Mr Teacherson exclaimed, pointing out the obvious.

The Spinosaurus thought the strange animal it was trying to eat was running away. So it gave chase.

Katie Menace grabbed hold of something, to

try to stop herself tumbling around inside the bus. It was the steering wheel.

The bus continued to roll, and for a brief moment the bus was back on its wheels. CLUMPH!

Katie landed in the driver's seat and quickly buckled herself in. The bus continued to roll, and before long Katie was sitting in a seat upside down, on the ceiling.

CLUMPH!

The bus rolled over a train track. Mr Teacherson knew it had as he saw it through the window his face was now squashed

up against. Thankfully the window didn't break, and the bus continued to roll.

CLUMPH! As it turned over, Mr Teacherson's view changed to that of the huge, gaping mouth of the Spinosaurus.

Mr Teacherson screamed. The mouth was so big it filled the window. Then as the bus rolled once more – **CLUMPH!** – all that he could see was sky.

At the front, through the leaves, Katie glimpsed an old-fashioned cobbled road, and realised the engine was still running.

CLUMPH!

The bus crashed onto the road, right way up, but only for a moment. The road was flat, but the momentum tipped the bus diagonally. For a moment, the bus balanced on two wheels.

"Everyone over on my side!" Katie shouted. Everyone clambered to the driver's side, and the extra weight helped the wobbling bus fall back onto its wheels.

CLUMPH!

As the Spinosaurus crashed through the bushes behind them, its jaws wide, Katie stamped on the accelerator and the bus tore off up the road. The Spino snapped its teeth together, missing the school bus by millimetres.

Lying on the floor in the bus, it took a moment for Mr Teacherson to realise he wasn't the one who was driving.

"Katie Menace!" he said sternly, as he sat up and looked out of the back window at the Spinosaurus. "Keep your foot down!"

THE VICTORIANS WERE HERE BEFORE US. IN VICTORIAN TIMES.

Mr Teacherson clambered to his feet and made his way to the front of the speeding bus. He glanced back. The Spinosaurus was nowhere to be seen.

"Ease up a bit, Katie. We're out of danger," he told the little Miss Menace.

"Should Katie really be driving?" asked Perry Panic. "She's only 10!"

"It's fine," Mr Teacherson replied. "It's illegal to drive on the Queen's highway without a licence, but these are private roads."

"It wasn't a legal question," Perry shouted. "It was a safety question!"

"How are there roads here to begin with?" Katie asked, ignoring Perry.

"The Victorians came to Duck Island," Mr Teacherson explained.

"When?"

"In Victorian times. They discovered the dinosaurs here and tried to build a dinosaur-themed park. Look, up ahead. There's a tourist information centre."

Katie saw the derelict, overgrown, long-abandoned tourist information centre, jerked the

Can you help Katie, Mr Teacherson and the class get to the middle of the island? The school bus is near the arrow on the map. The middle is the cross.

46

wheel to one side and drove the bus through it. She didn't want to stop when there might still be a hungry dinosaur chasing after them – plus, this was fun. As the bus barrelled through the gift shop, Brenda managed to grab a toy T. rex and Mr Teacherson grabbed a map.

"This'll be handy," he said. "We need to make our way to the centre of the island. So, er..."

The map wasn't hugely helpful. Different locations on it were numbered, but the bit of the map that explained what those numbers were had ripped off when Mr Teacherson grabbed it.

Finally, after what can only be described as an amazing adventure full of near misses and narrow escapes, Katie Menace got the bus to the centre of Duck Island.

"Stop the flashback!" Dennis shouted. "That's what I do in English when I get bored. You've pretty much just said, 'Then some stuff happened, the end!'."

"I thought you'd like to see the asteroid at the middle of the island, which keeps everything on Duck Island small," said Gran, showing Dennis a photo. It was of the class standing next to the asteroid, which seemed to be at the centre of a machine.

"What's all that junk on it?" Dennis asked.

"The asteroid is cracked, but the Victorians built that junk around it to keep it together."

"Naw, totally not bothered about that,"

Dennis complained. "Go back to the dinosaurs!"

"The asteroid is really important," Gran pointed out. "If it ever broke, Duck Island would expand all across Beanotown. Maybe even the whole country!"

"Awesome..." said Dennis, imagining Beanotown full of dinosaurs. "Gran, wouldn't that be awesome?"

Gran was looking at the TV again. Beanotown's entire police force (both of them) was running after the Pterodactyl, which was headed back to Duck Island.

The TV camera spun back round to the reporter. "When asked to comment, the Mayor of Beanotown said... Er, well he didn't really say anything. He just rubbed his hands together and laughed in what can only be described as an evil way," she said into her mic.

"Oh dear," said Gran.

"What?" asked Dennis.

"Grown-ups. That's why our class trip was the last one to the island and why everyone agreed to keep the dinosaurs on Duck Island a dark secret."

"Yeah – great secret-keeping, Gran," Dennis said. "Every kid in town knows about Duck Island!"

"That's fine. Kids never really ruined anything," she said with a sad face. "Grown-ups know now. And I'll bet the Mayor has some sort of scheme that will ruin the dinos for everyone."

Gran went off to make another cup of tea. Things always seem a bit better with a cup of tea in your hand.

Dennis was torn. On the one hand, dinosaurs taking over Beanotown would be awesome – but on the other hand, grown-ups had a habit of ruining loads of stuff, like games and jokes and pranks. All the Mayor ever tried to do was make money and ruin the fun. Like that time he tried to sell the skate park and turn it into a toxic waste dump.

Dennis couldn't let the Mayor ruin

Beanotown's worst-kept and coolest secret. There were only two things Dennis was happy to learn more about – skateboard tricks and dinosaurs. He had to get down there and make sure Duck Island was alright.

"Come on, Gnasher," said Dennis. "We need to get to Duck Island!"

WE'VE BEEN MEMED!

Chief O'Reilly and Sergeant Slipper were trying to catch a creature they were afraid of. They'd run after the Pterodactyl until they got near it... then run away. In the end, they sort of followed it back to Duck Island, from a safe distance.

"We chased the beast to Duck Island!" Chief O'Reilly informed the Mayor over the phone.

"I can see that!" the Mayor replied. "The TV cameras followed you."

"Tell him we have it cornered on Duck Island. No – trapped! Say we've got it trapped on Duck Island," Sergeant Slipper advised Chief O'Reilly.

"I heard that!" the Mayor snapped. "There's already GIFs and memes all over the internet of you running away from the thing!"

Chief O'Reilly turned to Sergeant Slipper. "We've been memed."

"We have?" exclaimed Sergeant Slipper. "I didn't feel a thing. Not deadly, is it?"

The Mayor rolled his eyes so hard that Chief O'Reilly heard it over the phone.

"If you want something done right, do it yourself!" he said to himself, and hung up.

The Mayor had a head start on Dennis. In fact, he arrived at the park at the same time Gnasher thought, Humf.

Walter also had a head start. So Walter arrived

at the duck pond just as his father finished paying the boat rental guy. (This is a different boat rental guy, by the way.)

Walter looked around at the peaceful park, at the innocent bystanders going about their daily business. And he thought about how much fun it would be to have a pet flying reptile to terrify them and send them screaming for their lives.

"Planning a little trip to Duck Island, father?" Walter asked.

"Yes," said Mayor Wilbur.

"Need any company?" Walter asked.

"No," Wilbur answered.

"Shame..." replied Walter sarcastically. "It could have been a lovely father–son moment."

I'm going to have to take a small detour here to describe Wilbur and Walter's relationship. Because it's amazing.

They're father and son and they love each other very much.

But they are both evil and deceitful, so will betray each other in a heartbeat.

On more than one occasion, Wilbur had found himself tied up in a broom cupboard feeling mixed emotions – anger at his son for having stolen his latest dastardly plan and tying him up, and pride in his son for stealing his latest dastardly plan and tying him up. He would find himself thinking: Blast that horrible disloyal boy of mine! That awful, underhand... wonderful boy. What a chip off the old block!

Keep your friends close and your enemies closer, thought the Mayor, changing his mind. And your son closest of all!

"You're right," said Wilbur. "What a lovely father–son moment. Let's go!"

Mayor Wilbur said, "What you need to understand is, the millionaires and billionaires of the world will spend a fortune to come here and see a real-life Pterodactyl!"

"I understand money!" Walter said, thinking

about how he could just get people to give *him* money once he has a terrifying Pterodactyl pet.

With that, they rowed over to Duck Island. Well, actually they paid the new boat rental guy to do the rowing.

Five minutes later, the Mayor and Walter stepped off the boat.

"Is this not a little bit dangerous, Father? It is a reptile, after all."

"All we're doing is checking its location, Walter," said the Mayor. "Once we locate its nest, then we'll get someone else to risk their life capturing it. On an island this size it should only take us a minute or two."

And with that, they both stepped through the bushes into the island.

Walter and Wilbur viewed the huge vista before them.

"Okay, maybe longer than a couple of minutes," the Mayor admitted.

THE SHORT CHAPTER

Dennis and Gnasher stood on the shore of the duck pond. They needed to get across to Duck Island, but Dennis could see that the boat rental guy was sitting in a boat that was tied up next to the island.

"Hey, Boat Rental Guy!" he shouted. "I wanna rent a boat!"

"I've got a name, you know!" Boat Rental Guy shouted back.

"I don't care! Just rent me a boat!" Dennis called back.

"Not until you guess my name!" Boat Rental Guy called back.

"Is it Stinky McButtface?" Dennis asked.

"No…" said BRG.

"Is it Lord Stinksalot?" Dennis asked.

"NO!" shouted BRG.

"Is it—"

"I'm not listening!"

"IF A DINOSAUR IS CHASING YOU AND YOUR SON, YOU DON'T NEED TO RUN FASTER THAN THE DINOSAUR. YOU JUST NEED TO RUN FASTER THAN YOUR SON!"

Despite its fearsome, many-horned appearance, the Triceratops is a peace-loving, herbivorous dinosaur. A vegetarian. It never uses its horns to attack, only in defence.

But there was something about the Mayor and Walter that got its back up straight away. They were instantly annoying!

"Arrrrrgh!" Walter screamed, as they ran through the jungle. "I thought Triceratopses were vegetarians!"

"Tell *him* that!" Walter's father shouted over his shoulder.

Just when Walter didn't think he could

possibly run any faster, one of the Triceratops's horns poked his butt.

Walter ran faster. Straight past his dad.

He's abandoning me! Wilbur thought. I'm so proud!

Walter dived through some bushes...

... into the boat on the shore.

"Floor it!" he shouted at the boat rental guy.

"This is a boat," BRG said. "You can't 'floor' boats, there's no accelerator. What about your dad?"

"Forget him!" Walter shouted. "He's—"

Just then, the Mayor dived out of the bushes and into the boat.

"Floor it!" the Mayor shouted at BRG.

"Like I said," BRG answered, "this is a boat. You can't—"

"Just shut up and row!" the Mayor said. BRG did as he was told.

The Triceratops hadn't followed them because it had done what it had wanted, which was to run them off the island. There could have been a good reason for this, like the Triceratops knew they were evil and would want to exploit and ruin the island, but there wasn't. It just didn't like them.

"Can't the army help?" Walter asked. Just as the boat reached the other shore. (The one that Dennis and Gnasher were standing on.)

"Yes!" his father agreed. "Let *them* take all the risks!"

Army? thought Dennis, as Walter and Wilbur climbed out of the boat, ignoring Dennis. What does he want the army to do? Dennis looked to Gnasher and said, "Whatever it is, it can't be good. We should get over there and keep an eye on them"

"I could do with a cup of tea, Helen," the Mayor said, as they strode out of the park.

Walter looked at his dad with a quizzical look. Wilbur looked around. He'd forgotten to bring his tea maker with him.

PINK TANK

"CLOTT, YOU BLITHERING BUFFOON!" shouted Colonel Grumbly. **"WHY IS BERTHA'S TANK PINK?!"**

Corporal Clott squinted at the bright-pink tank. He couldn't see what was wrong with it. But he could see that Corporal Bertha, who was standing in the gun turret, was fuming.

"This is a modern, up-to-date army, Clott!" Colonel Grumbly informed him. "We've moved with the times. We don't paint our tanks pink for girls and blue for boys. We paint them green!"

Clott was suddenly worried. He'd forgotten what Colonel Grumbly had said at the start of his shouting, and now he wasn't listening to what he was currently shouting. He tried to tune back in...

"Not because green is gender neutral, but because it blends in!"

"SIR, YES SIR!" Clott shouted. Clott had figured out, long ago, that if he shouted "SIR, YES SIR!" when Colonel Grumbly was shouting at him, the Colonel would usually stop. At least until the next time he did something wrong.

"Now repaint it **green!**" Colonel Grumbly ordered.

"Aye aye, your majesty!" Clott saluted and picked up a pot of fresh paint. Colonel Grumbly turned bright red. "What are you going to do with that?!" Clott looked at the pot of paint in his hands. It felt like a trick question. Could he say **"SIR, YES SIR!"** again? "I, er..."

Colonel Grumbly squinted at Clott. "Are you colour blind, corporal?" he asked.

"Yes! Completely!" Clott replied with a huge grin on his face.

Colonel Grumbly sighed and held his head in his hands. "That's fine," he said quietly. "Nothing wrong in that. I myself have trouble with my blues and greens..."

His voice was increasing in volume now.

"THAT'S WHY I... READ THE TIN!" he shouted. **"IT'S GOT THE COLOUR WRITTEN ON IT!"**

The Colonel jabbed the tin in Clott's hands, right where it read Luminous Orange.

Colonel Grumbly's phone rang. **"WHAT?!"** he answered.

Two miles away, the Mayor fell over with a sore ear.

"This is the Mayor!" the Mayor shouted back. "Get over to the duck pond as fast as you can. Bring everything you need to build a secure base."

"Er... sorry, Mayor!" Colonel Grumbly said.

"Of course sir. Straight away sir!"

By this time, Dennis was already halfway to the army base. He'd overheard the Mayor saying he was going to call the army, so figured that was the best place to go to see what Wilbur's plan might be.

"My mate Will's house backs onto the army base," Dennis said to Gnasher as they ran. "He'll help me get in somehow. Then maybe we can find out what the Mayor has planned."

Will saved his game, stood up and adjusted the belt of his mum's fluffy dressing gown. Grabbing his cup of Earl Grey, he smiled at his guest and strode out into the garden.

He pointed up to the tree at the back of the garden, with his non-tea-holding hand.

"If you climb that tree, you'll be able to see into the base," Will told... Minnie.

(I bet you thought he was talking to Dennis.)

"Some of the branches grow out over the fence. You should be able to get in that way." He took a huge slurp of tea. "Ooh, that's lovely, that is!"

"What are you doing here?" Dennis shouted from behind them.

Will raised an eyebrow. "I live here!"

"Not you!" said Dennis. He pointed at Minnie. "Her!"

"I saw this awesome mutant seagull on the telly," Minnie explained. "And I thought I'm having that for a pet. They always send the army after mutants in movies, so I thought I'd best get round to Will's 'cos his garden backs onto the base!"

"It's not a mutant seagull. It's a Pterodactyl! Why not just go straight to the island yourself?" Dennis asked.

Minnie rolled her eyes and started climbing the tree. "How am I gonna catch one of them?!" she asked. "Much easier to let someone else capture it for me, then pinch it."

Dennis didn't know what to say. Minnie's plan was actually pretty smart. And he needed to beat her to it! So he chased after her, closely followed by Gnasher.

Will took another slurp of tea. "Never seen a dog climb a tree before!"

HONEY BADGER

From high in the tree, Dennis, Gnasher and Minnie could see the whole base, (and also hear someone in the distance shouting about the importance of reading the labels on things).

"Why are you here, anyway?" asked Minnie.

"I'm saving the dinosaurs!" Dennis replied, prodding his chest. "The Mayor's planning to sell them all or something. He could destroy Duck Island and all its secrets!"

He then prodded Minnie in the arm.

"You're just going to pinch one to be your pet!"

"And?" Minnie replied.

"And, so when this is over you gotta tell everyone how awesome I was!" Dennis was thinking if he was going to do the right thing everyone should know.

You may be thinking, at this point: Walter

wants a Pterodactyl as a pet, but Walter's evil. Why's it alright for Minnie to have a Pterodactyl as a pet?

Well it's not. Some animals don't make good pets. My parents got a honey badger when I was a kid. It's a cute name and they're only small, but they're the toughest, angriest, most fearless animal on Earth.

When Mum said to me, "Nigel, we've got you a honey badger," I was overjoyed, for two

seconds. Right before we all got chased out of the house by the cute, furious, fluffy, vicious creature.

It was unbelievably angry with me and my parents, for no reason. Dad tried to fend it off with a chair, but that was quickly turned to sawdust. "Everybody out!" he screamed, before turning round to find we'd left him in there.

We had to find a new house. The honey badger still lives there now, at number 32!

There's also a difference in the way Walter and Minnie would treat a pet Pterodactyl. Walter would put the thing into serious intensive training, forcing it to learn complicated tricks. He'd also keep it in a tiny cage, whereas Minnie would just say, "Look! I got a dinosaur bird. Her name is Clarabelle," and she'd let it sleep wherever it wanted, and feed it burgers.

Over on the far side of the base, it looked like

the army were packing up to leave, and it looked like they'd be finished soon. Amphibious trucks and troop transporters were getting loaded with all sorts of gubbins. (Amphibious vehicles can drive through water and even float.)

"We need to get on one of those boat-trucks!" Minnie said.

"How?" asked Dennis. "Look at all the cameras!"

Finally, Dennis, Gnasher and Minnie made it across, without setting off any of the motion detectors. They crouched low, peeking round the corner at the almost fully loaded army trucks. There were only a few moments left to stow away.

They heard the shouty voice of Colonel Grumbly nearby.

"And while I've got you here, Clott..." he shouted. "You've done a rubbish job of installing the movement detectors. None of them work! You can do star jumps in front of any of them and

Can you find a way to the tank for Dennis and Minnie?

74

the base alarm still doesn't go off!"

Dennis rolled his eyes while, behind him, Minnie did star jumps in front of one of the motion detectors they'd just spent ages trying to avoid.

While Colonel Grumbly was shouting at Corporal Clott, Dennis, Minnie and Gnasher took advantage of the distraction, dodged across to the nearest vehicle and stowed away...

ALL THE TROMBONES

It wasn't long before Dennis, Gnasher and Minnie were hiding inside a cramped storage box onboard one of the trucks, and the convoy was on its way to Duck Island.

"Get your stinky foot out of my face!" Dennis complained.

"That's your foot!" said Minnie.

Dennis tried to feel the foot in question but couldn't move his arms enough, so he bit it instead.

"Ow!" he said.

The truck stopped.

"Are we there yet?" Minnie asked.

The storage box opened and a face peered in.

"Hello!" said Corporal Clott, like they were friends, not stowaways. "We're here!"

"Hello. We're, er..." Dennis started.

"Here to see the dinosaur island?" asked Clott, like that was just fine.

"Yes?" said Dennis, not understanding why this army man wasn't super cross.

Dennis, Minnie and Gnasher unfolded themselves out of the box.

Dennis turned to Minnie. "So, er, now we need to..."

"You don't have a heroic plan to save your dino chums from the evil Mayor's clutches, do you?" Minnie said.

"Yeah I do!" Dennis protested. "I'm, er... "

"What's going on in here?" Colonel Grumbly asked as he poked his head into the truck.

"They're here to see the island, your lordship!" Clott said proudly.

"Stowaways..." said Grumbly. "You can't just let anyone on army manoeuvres, Clott! **OUT! ALL OF YOU!**"

Outside, Dennis, Minnie and Gnasher blinked in the bright sunlight. The army trucks were parked in a large half circle, in front of a large Victorian mansion... surrounded by jungle.

"Aw cool!" said Dennis, gawping at the towering building. "The Victorians must have built it when they were trying to turn the island into a dinosaur park."

Minnie was looking at the jungle. She'd noticed an odd-looking tree trunk growing up out of it. It had no branches whatsoever, and disappeared into the low lying cloud above them.

Dennis looked across the clearing and saw Walter and his father. Things were gonna get boring if they saw him so Dennis did his best "blending into the background" so as not to get noticed.

Walter and his Dad suddenly looked directly at Dennis and co climbing out of the truck.

But before anyone could do anything, everyone and everything around them was shaken by the loudest, most incredible noise they'd ever heard.

"BLARP!"

The noise came from everywhere around them. It sounded like trumpets and tubas and trombones. All the trumpets and tubas and trombones that there are in the world.

The branchless tree trunk that Minnie had seen earlier started to slowly fall over and... bend? The giant head of a Titanosaurus lowered from the clouds, into camp. It grabbed Corporal Bertha and threw her into the jungle.

Minnie had been looking at a dinosaur and

hadn't realised. It had been standing right next to camp, and no one had seen it!

"BLARP!"

The Titanosaur's neck shook and vibrated with the sound, its neck acting like an incredibly long horn.

The dinosaur was so huge that you couldn't see all of it at once. You could choose to look up and up and up at its head. Or down to a huge tree trunk leg. Or look over to another leg.

Everybody screamed and ran in different directions. A dark shape flitted through, in-between the vehicles. Then another. Then another. Dennis only saw one for less than a second, but that was all he needed to recognise the familiar shape. **RAPTORS!** The three raptors rushed into the middle of the camp. Grinning like naughty children.

One of the huge Titanosaur tree trunk legs uprooted itself and moved closer into camp.

Bertha landed in a tree and quickly decided to stay there.

BOOM! The Titanosaur placed a foot down, and the ground shook.

Dennis barrelled up the crumbling stone steps of the Victorian mansion, but the door was locked. It was the weirdest lock he'd ever seen – it was like an ancient phone, with a fancy handle and spaces for letters along the top.

BOOM! As the Titanosaur took another

step, the house shook and tiles fell off the roof.

Gnasher gave Dennis one of his best "Hurry up!" looks.

Dennis looked over his shoulder.
Most of the army people had locked themselves into the trucks. The Mayor and Walter couldn't be seen anywhere.

Dennis looked down. There was a skeleton near his feet, wearing fancy Victorian clothes.

This guy obviously knew the word, but only got the first two letters in before he was chomped! thought Dennis.

He looked over his shoulder again. One of the raptors was standing on one of the trucks, looking right at him! It hopped down to the ground.

Arrrrgh! thought Dennis. What's the rest of this word?! It was obvious that once the word was in, the door would open, but how was Dennis meant to know what that was? It began D, A...

"BLARP!"

That noise was making it really hard to think.

Suddenly he knew.

Dennis had seen a weird eight-letter word earlier that day. (So have you.) And now the fancy handle made sense!

Gnasher gave Dennis his best "That dinosaur is getting really close!" look. Dennis dialled the next letter, and it flipped up to replace the question mark.

In movies whenever someone is trying to guess a password on a computer they try words that are connected to whoever's computer it is. The computer owner's cat's name, things like that. This had to be something similar. But Dennis had hardly been on the island. Hadn't seen much of it. Didn't know enough to guess. If Gran had been there, she would have probably have been able to guess something from her school trip. Dennis realised he'd seen pictures from the school trip!

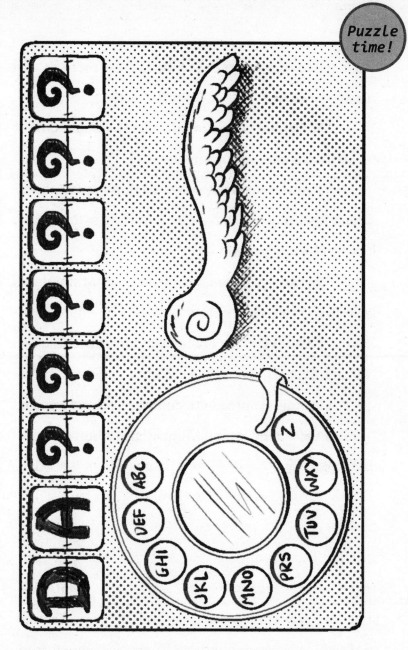

Can you figure out this word by looking back at the story so far?

Daedalus

85

He tried to remember the pictures. Was there a word in any of them?

You could go back to the chapter about Gran's school visit and look yourself...

The door opened, and Dennis and Gnasher dived inside.

"Come on, Min—"

Suddenly Dennis realised that Minnie was nowhere to be seen either!

BOOM! The Titanosaur took another step. Plaster dust fell from the ceiling.

Dennis slammed the door shut behind him and said to Gnasher, "I hope Minnie hasn't been eaten!"

This dinosaur looks boring. All the most fashionable animals are covered in spots, stripes or other shapes. Give this dino a cool pattern.

OTHER THINGS TO WORRY ABOUT

I hope Dennis has been eaten! Minnie thought to herself as she ran through the jungle.

"BLARP!"

The sound of the ridiculously enormous dinosaur wasn't quite so loud, now that she was running away.

As Minnie ran, she looked back over her shoulder. The raptor that had been chasing her wasn't there anymore either. Score!

SNAP! The creature lunged at her through the foliage,

snapping its jaws. Okay, maybe it was still chasing her!

Minnie ran faster. Time for plan B.

She grabbed branches, pulling them back and letting go, so that they'd flick back and slap the raptor in the face.

Only that didn't happen. Raptors are great at dodging things, you see. It was still hot on her heels.

Plan C was to, er... er... There was no plan C!

Suddenly, what looked like a half-sized T. rex burst out of the jungle to Minnie's left. The raptor snapped at it, in a "Get off, that's my dinner!" kind of way.

The fully grown Abelisaurus just, straight up, tried to eat the raptor. The raptor only just managed to get away, falling in the scramble. The Abelisaurus snapped again. Lying on its side, the raptor kicked it as it came in for a chomp. The kick made the Abelisaurus twist its head and for a second it was looking right at Minnie. Which is when Minnie realised she should have been running instead of watching the cool dino fight. The Abelisaurus looked back to the raptor. The raptor had (wisely) gone. The Abelisaurus looked back to Minnie, who was running away.

Running forwards, but looking back, screaming, Minnie ran off a cliff...

... and fell into a river.

She should have known. So far, today had definitely felt like an awesome action movie, (hint, hint, Hollywood, if you're reading) and people who fall off cliffs in movies always fall into rivers.

At least I got away from that din... Minnie thought, before the Abelisaurus fell into the river in front of her.

"**URRRGH!** Give me a break!" she shouted at the sky.

Instead of a break, however, life presented Minnie with a waterfall. She heard the rumble first, then saw the river ahead drop away into a splashy mist.

Something else you discover in movies is that behind every waterfall there's a secret cave. Because that's really cool.

I wonder if there's a cave behind this waterfall I'm about to go over, she thought. Wait! Waterfall!!!

SNAP! The Abelisaurus tried to bite her.

"Mate! We've got other things to worry about," Minnie shouted, pointing at the fast-approaching waterfall.

SNAP! SNAP! It tried again to chomp Minnie, but this only caused it roll over in the churning water.

Minnie saw her chance. As the dinosaur

turned belly up, Minnie scrambled up onto its tummy and got to her feet.

The outraged dinosaur continued to roll, however, snapping its jaws underwater.

Minnie saw a low-lying tree branch and jumped to grab it, just as the Abelisaurus's head surfaced again.

SNAP! SNAP! SNAP!

It tried to bite Minnie's dangling legs three more times, before it slid over the waterfall and plunged into the churning waters below.

Minnie hung there for a moment before saying, "Cool!" Then she pulled herself up and climbed along the branch until she was over land.

As she dropped to the grass, she wondered if the dinosaur that had tried so hard to eat her was okay.

(It was. It was fine. Just thought you'd like to know.)

THE BLIGHTER'S OVER
HERE, OR HEREABOUTS.

Dennis and Gnasher were in a huge room. The house was built on the edge of a slope so, while they'd come in on the ground floor at the front, here at the back they were upstairs. The roof was glass. And the room itself was full of dinosaurs!

Statues of dinosaurs.

Dennis stepped in. It was like the most awesome museum display ever. Or, at least, it had been at one time. The glass ceiling was full of holes. The rain had been pouring in for years. Several of the full-size dinosaur models were falling apart. Some were missing, like it had been abandoned before being properly finished. Next to most of these were information boards, though on many the text had long since washed away.

In amongst the statues, Dennis spotted a full-size raptor model that seemed to be in good condition, so he moved over to it. It was very lifelike. Whoever'd made it was good at their job. It was so realistic, it almost looked like it was breathing. He could just make out the last few sentences on the sign next to it.

"Hey Gnasher, listen to this. It says here that raptors are highly intelligent, and that their complex calls mean they could one day be capable of simple speech."

Dennis looked up at the model of the raptor.

"What does that mean?" he wondered. "Talking like a parrot, or proper talking?"

The raptor turned to meet his gaze and said, in a posh Victorian accent, "If you ask me, that sounds like a load of nonsense, old bean!"

"ARRRGH!" One of the statues wasn't a statue. It was real! Dennis stumbled back, fell onto his butt then quickly flipped over and scrambled for cover, behind a fake Triceratops.

The raptor hopped down from the display, as two more raptors entered the room.

"Clarence, my dear boy!" called one. "You haven't seen a rather scruffy looking urchin around here, have you?"

It was the raptor who'd been staring at Dennis outside – it must have followed him in somehow.

"I have indeed, Fletcher," Clarence replied. "The blighter's over here, or hereabouts!"

Dennis couldn't believe what he was hearing.

These dinosaurs could speak, and they could speak better than him!

The floor under him was soaking. The glass ceiling above him had a huge hole in it. It must have been raining in for at least a hundred years. The wood under his hands felt spongy.

Dennis crawled toward the left side wall, hoping to spot a way out. He was worried about Gnasher too. Where was he?

The raptor called Clarence jumped up onto the display Dennis was hiding behind. Dennis looked up to see him loom over him.

Then there was an odd, wet creak and the rotted floor beneath him gave way.

CLANG! KUNG! CLANG! went Dennis, as he bounced off a cooker hood, onto and off a cooker, and down onto the basement floor below.

Gnasher saw Dennis fall and was just about to run after him when he saw a large, black, furry shape outside...

Dennis was in a large kitchen.

"I hope they didn't hear that!" Dennis whispered to himself.

"Hard not to, my dear boy!" said one of raptors, peering down through the hole in the ceiling. "You're louder than a Titanosaur with a trombone, I'm afraid!"

With a delicate hop, it dropped down through the hole Dennis had just made, and into the kitchen.

Dennis grabbed a pan and threw it, but the raptor dodged it so easily you'd think it had been thrown in slow motion.

"Are you going to eat me for dinner, like you did all the guys who built this place?" Dennis asked.

"I haven't eaten anybody yet!" said the offended raptor. "All that bad business was more

than a hundred years ago. That was my great-great-grandmother."

Another raptor hopped down.

"You're not going to eat me, then?" Dennis asked.

"No, we will – but don't take it personally. You seem like a decent chap," Clarence conceded. "But we've seen what you humans have done to the rest of the world, and we'd rather you didn't do it here."

Dennis picked up a jar as big as a waste paper bin and held it above his head.

"Grown-ups messed the planet up. Not me! I'm here to stop the Mayor. I'm here to save you guys!"

"Do I look like I need saving?" said Fletcher.

The jar above Dennis's head popped open and its contents spla-ooshed out.

"Aw, come on!" cried Dennis. "Gimme a break!"

The raptors sniffed.

"Is that barbecue sauce?" asked Fletcher.

HONK!

At this exact time, Walter and Wilbur were hopelessly lost in the jungle. They'd done bit of running, but they'd quickly slowed to a walk.

"New plan!" the Mayor announced to his son. "This whole dinosaur park thing seems doomed to failure. The island is far too big – and dangerous! Once we find a way off the island, we stay off it forever!"

"I'm liking this plan so far, Father."

"Once we're home, I'll charge millionaire hunters a million pounds a day to come here and hunt dinosaurs."

"Paid for in advance, just in case the hunters don't make it back?" suggested Walter.

"Excellent suggestion!" the Mayor replied, beaming with pride.

I don't think I'm spoiling things too much by saying that the hunting thing doesn't happen. No dinosaurs were harmed in the making of this book.

But the Mayor does get eaten.

Ha! Ha! No, he doesn't. This book is like a 12A movie. There might be a few edgy bits, but no one's going to get eaten.

Or are they?

(Yes, they are. The Mayor.)

"A Sarahsaurus," said Walter. "There. Look!"

Walter was pointing at a small dinosaur no bigger than a sheep. It looked like a tiny Diplodocus, only somehow it was on two feet.

"Is that a meat-eater?" asked the Mayor.

"No," Walter answered. "I don't think so."

The creature put its front two limbs down. It seemed comfortable on either two or four legs.

"You'd better know so!" Wilbur said. "Those teeth look sharp."

"I'm pretty sure..."

"Grab it then!" the Mayor told his son. "We can take it back with us and use it in an advert!"

They inched towards the animal, and pounced at the same time. Walter grabbed the head end and Wilbur grabbed the tail end.

The Sarahsaurus honked like a goose. A distressed, "Help, I don't like this!" sort of a honk.

"HONK!"

Wilbur and Walter laughed.

"HONK! HONK! HONK!" went the Sarahsaurus, and the Mayor and his son laughed even more.

"HONK! HONK!..."

"HONK!"

The Mayor and his son stopped laughing. That last honk had come from behind them, and it wasn't a "Help, I don't like this!" sort of honk. It was an angry "Put my baby down!" sort of honk.

They turned around, the young Sarahsaurus still wriggling in their arms.

Fully grown Sarahsauruses are a bit bigger than the one they had hold of. About the size of a cow. And there were two of them.

"I think I remember a bit more about Sarahsauruses, now," Walter said, as he and his father slowly put the baby down. Their eyes were fixed on the parent dinosaurs. "They are, in fact, mostly vegetarian."

But Wilbur was already running, trying to get a head start on his son.

In a heart-warming, tender moment the Sarahsaurus mother comforted her baby.

Less heart-warming was the male adult who chased after Walter, honking and snapping at him.

Walter crashed through the bushes into a clearing and saw his dad on a little train platform, diving into a steam train.

The Mayor slammed the door shut.

"I could really do with a cup of tea," the Mayor said to himself. "Why didn't I bring Helen?!"

DINNER TIME!

"Urrrgh!" Dennis groaned, then sniffed, "It *is* barbecue sauce!"

Dennis's phone rang.

The raptors all looked at him with puzzled looks. They almost seemed afraid.

Dennis gently set the jar he'd been holding down on the bench next to him and reached into his pocket. He was surprised phones worked here. It felt like he was on a tropical island 10,000 miles away from home – but he was actually, sort of, still in the park.

Pulling out his phone – actually his mum's old phone that she insisted he carry, "just in case"– he held up a finger to the raptors and said, "Just a minute." Then, into the phone: "Hello?"

"Dinner's going to be ready in 20 minutes, love," said Mum, on the other end.

Dennis looked at the raptors.

"I'm a little busy, Mum," he told her.

"It's sausage and mash. I suppose it'll keep in the oven." She sighed. "Don't be too late back. Have fun with your friends!"

Sausage?! thought Gnasher. "We gneed to escape the island!" The threat of being eaten by raptors hadn't bothered Gnasher, but the idea of missing out on sausages was very worrying indeed!

Dennis looked at the raptors. They didn't look all that friendly.

"Your mother's right," said one of the raptors. "It is dinner time."

CRASH!

It sounded like something had been smashed to bits in the next room. A second later, Gnasher's enormous head came round the corner.

No, that's wrong. It wasn't Gnasher's head at all. This was the Gnashersaurus rex!

Dennis recognized it immediately, as its body came into view. The gigantic dinosaur was crouching as it came around the corner, snapping and gnashing as it did.

Everyone darted off in different directions. Actual Gnasher (the dog) appeared behind the Gnashersaurus rex.

"Gnash, gnash, gnash, gnash!" he said to the much larger, pre-historic version of himself, which meant, "Mate, don't eat Dennis! We're here to save him!" Earlier, Gnasher had spotted the Gnashersaurus rex out of the window and had persuaded him to come and help, for old time's sake. But was his plan about to backfire completely?

"GNASH!" gnashed the Gnashersaurus rex, snapping at Gnasher and almost catching him.

"Gnash, gnash, gnash?!" said Gnasher, which meant, "Who's side are you on?!"

I should explain here that Gnashersauruses are temperamental creatures, with short memories. For example, you can hatch a plan with one to save your friend from raptor-based doom, but in all the excitement it can forget the plan and try to eat the very human you're trying to save!

But while everyone was looking at the Gnashersaurus rex, Dennis disappeared out through a side door.

He had fallen down one floor when he fell into the kitchen, so Dennis knew the front door was one floor up. But where were the stairs?

He spotted a sign saying **EXIT** that had an arrow pointing the same way he was running.

Finally, he thought, some good luck!

Then, through the gloom, he saw a lift at the end of the corridor with a sign above it that read **WAY OUT**. Get in! thought Dennis, and raced into the open lift, closely followed by Gnasher. "Gnasher!" Dennis exclaimed. "Where've you been?"

Gnasher was overjoyed to see Dennis and jumped up to lick his face.

"Alright! Alright!" Dennis laughed. "I'm glad to see you too!"

But Gnasher kept licking him. Under the chin, behind the ears, in the ears...

"Hey!" said Dennis. "Are you happy to see me, or is this because I'm covered in barbecue sauce?"

Gnasher licked his lips and gave Dennis his best "Push the 'up' button!" look.

Just as he spotted two raptors at the far end of the corridor, Dennis pushed the 'up' button.

Nothing happened.

Dennis pressed the 'up' button 78 more times in the next three seconds, but still nothing happened.

There were three raptors now, and they were heading slowly towards the lift. It didn't look like they'd seen Dennis and Gnasher yet, but in a few more steps they would.

In desperation, Dennis read the note that was taped above the buttons. It was about how the lift didn't work properly. Great.

Dennis could see now that the wiring panel was hanging off and that a lot of the wires inside were broken. He would need a complete wire to make the lift move. There was a slider at the bottom, so you could choose between the six wires.

The raptors were nearer.

Any second now they were going to...

BOOOOSH! The wall just behind the raptors exploded as the Gnashersaurus rex crashed through.

The raptors ran. They ran as quickly as they could in the only direction they could – towards Dennis!

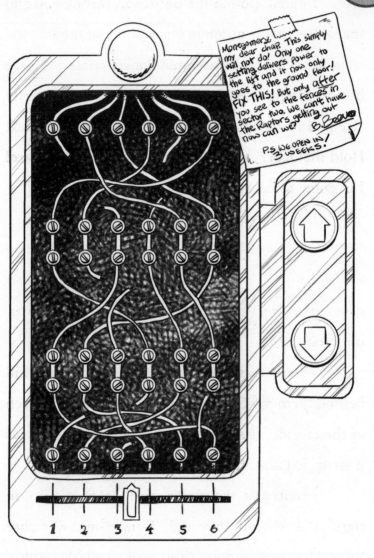

Can you figure out the right number to make the lift go?

Dennis spotted the unbroken setting and slid the slider to that number.

Fletcher, the lead raptor saw Dennis and gave him a complicated look... It seemed to be partly "Help, I'm being chased by a Gnashersaurus rex! Hold the door!" and partly "HA HA! There you are! I'm going to eat you!"

Dennis pressed the 'up' button.

The lift doors did not close instantly, which was what Dennis kinda needed them to do. Instead they closed frighteningly slowly, with a long, drawn-out creeeeeeeak!

The raptors were now horrifyingly close, and behind them the Gnashersaurus rex filled every inch of the corridor. Its head scraped along the ceiling as it struggled after them.

Eventually the doors clanged shut, just in time. The second they did, Dennis and Gnasher heard the three raptors thud against them. With a clunk, the lift went up.

"Phew!" said Dennis. "We're safe."

Gnasher agreed, slumping to the floor.

Unfortunately, Dennis was wrong about that.

MINNIE?

The Mayor wasn't happy.

He was safe now, inside the train – but it was a Victorian train. There was plenty of coal on board, but this had to be shovelled into the boiler and lit just to get the train moving. And this coal-shovelling looked an awful lot like work.

"Let me in!" Walter urged, knocking on the door slightly faster than is humanly possible.

Maybe Walter could do some shovelling, thought the Mayor.

"OPEN THIS DOOR, FATHER!" Walter screamed, **"OR I'LL HAVE MY REVENGE!"**

Wilbur opened the door, and Walter fell in. They slammed the door shut behind them and a second later the daddy Sarahsaurus bashed into the train door.

Walter and Wilbur heard a distant horn.

Dinosaurs seemed to make some odd sounds,

but this was almost certainly a horn. Not a car or bike horn – the sort of horn you blow through.

The sound came again, nearer this time. What was it? There was a background rumble now too, like thunder.

Looking outside, Wilbur could see that the dinosaur outside had gone. Had the noise scared it away?

They heard the horn again, loud, just as a Viking longboat sailed into view. Stood at the front, blowing a horn, was Minnie the Minx.

"Minnie?" Thought Wilbur and Walter. (And me when I first heard.)

Just in case you think maybe you missed a bit – there wasn't a stream or river crossing in front of the train. It was just land. But all the same a longboat sailed across, on wheels made of round Viking shields.

The boat crashed past, but the general background rumble didn't lessen, not until the two Allosauruses chasing it also crashed past in front of the train.

Walter's mouth fell wide open with shock, but the Mayor looked unimpressed and handed his son a spade.

PING!

Dennis and Gnasher stood in the lift, waiting for it to reach the level above.

"It should be quick," said Dennis to Gnasher. "The note said the lift only goes to the ground floor."

The lights above the door showed that they had now reached ground floor, but the lift didn't stop.

"Up one more?" said Dennis. The next light above the door lit up. **"TWO?!"** The lift wasn't stopping. "**ARGH!** The wiring's so messed up we could be stopping at any floor!"

PING! Some time later, the doors opened with a creak. Dennis and Gnasher peeked out.

They were on the top floor.

At some point after the note had been written, the wiring must have been changed to make it go up to the small, round, cluttered office they were now in.

Dennis looked around. The room's most striking features were the domed ceiling and the big hole in it.

"We must be in the tower," Dennis said to Gnasher. "This looks like the boss's office."

Books and papers littered the floor. Dennis picked one up. It was a design. The drawing showed a Titanosaur with a carriage on its back. The idea must have been to use a tame Titanosaur to give

people rides. The drawing was signed B. Beano, same as the note from the lift.

B. Beano? Dennis thought.

He knew from school that the town was founded in some year starting with an 18, by the Beano brothers. They were toymakers. Barry and Brian.

Barry had been the odd one, the toy designer who'd also designed the old bit of the town. This included the town hall and its clock tower, which had turned out to be a time machine. They hadn't told Dennis about the clock tower in school. That had been something he'd figured out himself.

This was probably Barry's office.

It was the luxury office of a big boss. It was proper, not like the manager's office at WIDL or Jeff's office at Jeff's Auto Repair and Aquarium. This was the real deal!

On the desk in the middle of the room were drawings and plans for all kinds of awesome dinosaur attractions. A Mythological Maze design caught Dennis's eye, with the statue of Daedalus at its entrance. Instead of a Minotaur, Barry had planned to keep the Spinosaurus inside it. Had that maze ever been built though? There weren't any photos of it in Gran's album, only one picture of the statue.

In among all the notes and sketches, Dennis found a diary.

He opened it at a random page and read:

As well as dinosaurs, this island seems to have collected important things from every stage of Earth's history. Yesterday, we found a Spitfire plane. The pyramid near the volcano is almost certainly a genuine construct...

Dennis skipped ahead.

...Triceratops may not be meat eaters, but that doesn't stop them being incredibly grumpy! The damage they've done to the fences in sector...

Dennis skipped ahead again.

The Vikings attacked the building site for the Pterodactyl cage again today. There's now no hope of getting ready in time for opening. I hate those guys!

Then, a few pages on:

Montgomery has noticed worrying cracks in the asteroid that keeps the island small. If it were to break apart, this would all be for nothing. I've instructed him to build something to keep this from happening.

Then, later:

Montgomery has taught a raptor how to speak. It's only a few words, but it should entertain the crowds. I doubt the animal understands what it's saying, but...

And, right at the end:

The raptors are far smarter than we realised. They escaped today, and tried to eat me! I've hidden up here in my office. From the window, I can see that my dream is now in ruins. I'll return to Beanotown and restart my work on Project Icarus. The

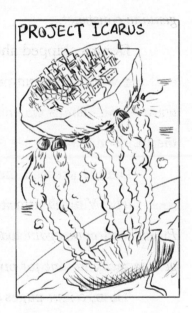

dinosaurs and Vikings can keep their stupid island! I'm going to use the cable car to escape to a place of safety. If I don't make it, perhaps one day someone will find this, and...

The mention of the cable car interested

Dennis. The broken lift only led back downstairs to the raptors, but the cable car had taken B. Beano to safety.

It took him a second to find it. Between two windows, there was a door. He tried it, but it wouldn't open.

Next to the door were lots of tiny, square buttons with dinosaur pictures on. Some of these were blank. There was obviously some sort of code to put in, but what?

Dennis pressed the empty button on the top row, next to the Triceratops. It lit up, as did four round buttons at the bottom. He pressed the T. rex button, and the lights went out.

"So the right dino will stay lit, I guess," Dennis said. But which was the right dino?

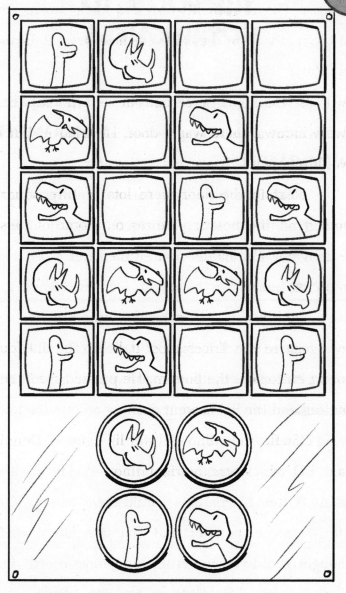

Can you figure it out, and complete the pattern before Dennis?

THE DOOR TO NOTHINGNESS

Just as Dennis figured it out – whoomph! – there came a worrying sound. **WHOOMPH! WHOOMPH!** It was moving nearer.

The office got a little darker as a Pterodactyl landed on the hole in the dome. Luckily it was looking out, and hadn't noticed them yet.

As quietly as he could, Dennis opened the door... and saw that the cable car wasn't there!

There was simply all of outside! There wasn't even a railing or anything to stop you falling out, just the cable above his head, stretching off into the low-lying cloud.

Dennis wasn't particularly good at health and safety. Often his parents would have to say, "Get off the garage roof!" or "Put that saw down!" or "I thought I told you to get off the garage roof?!" But these Victorians took it to a whole other level.

Now that the door to nothingness was open, Dennis could see a little button set into the door frame. The call button.

Even with his relaxed attitude to safety, Dennis thought to himself: Wouldn't it be better to have the call button on the inside? Then the cable car could come before you open the door.

Dennis pressed the button and the cable above him shook a little and started to move noisily. Would the sound draw the attention of the Pterodactyl on the roof?

Dennis turned, ready to fend off the winged beast, but the creature was quietly staring out to the jungle below.

This Pterodactyl's got bad hearing, Dennis thought. My luck's changed!

The cable car emerged from the mist. The closer it got, the more it clanged and pinged and dinged and shook the cable.

CLANG! CLANG! CLANG!

This was not a nice modern cable car made of steel and glass. This was more like a cage dangling from a wire. The bars were widely spaced too – they wouldn't be completely safe once inside it.

Dennis kept an eye on the Pterodactyl, but it hadn't moved.

"Not long now," Dennis whispered to Gnasher.

KUNG!!!

The cable car slammed into the side of the building, its door flung open, and the whole office shook.

"**BWALK!**" the Pterodactyl cried out. It heard and felt that! But it flapped its wings a couple of times and settled again.

Phew! thought Dennis.

BEEPITY BEEP BEEP DING DONG BEEP!

It was Dennis's phone – his mum was calling him again.

This sound enraged the Pterodactyl.

"BWALK! BWALK! BWALK!"

As Dennis fumbled in his pocket, the Pterodactyl wrenched its head round like an owl and glared at him.

Gnasher got on the cable car. Dennis ran in after and shut the door behind him, answering the phone as he did so.

"In the middle of a thing, Mum!" Dennis shouted into the phone.

"BWALK!" cried the Pterodactyl. It flapped down into the office.

"You still haven't had your dinner!" Dennis's mum replied.

"BWALK!"

The creature hopped forwards and jabbed its beak in between the bars of the cable car. Dennis dodged it and pressed the call button again. The cable car set off, moving away from the building.

"Where are you, Dennis? Are you round a friend's house watching action films again?"

The Pterodactyl launched itself into the air after them.

"Something like that!"

Mum groaned. "Right, well, I'll put it in the microwave. You can zap it, if you ever come back!"

She hung up, as the cable car slipped into the low-lying clouds. The jungle far below disappeared from view, and soon Dennis and Gnasher were utterly alone with the Pterodactyl.

Would they ever make it home for dinner?

LOOOOOSER

The situation was really getting to Gnasher. He was cornered, with nowhere to go.

"GNASH!" he gnashed at the flying reptile.

The Pterodactyl was shocked. It ate things this size. Those meals had never tried to eat him back! It let go of the cable car.

WHOOMPH! WHOOMPH! WHOOMPH!

The winged beast circled the cable car. As it swooped back towards them, Gnasher turned into a swirling, slavering mass of teeth and fur.

GNASH! GNASH! GNASH!

(It was actually a pretty good honey badger impression.)

The Pterodactyl instinctively ducked, and flew underneath them.

As it came back up, Gnasher gave it his best "Come on then. Try it!" look.

GNASH! GNASH!

At this, the Pterodactyl decided it was probably a good idea to get dinner somewhere else, and flew off.

"Phew," said Dennis, patting his dog. "Thanks, Gnasher! If Minnie does get one of those things as a pet, I'm never going round her place again."

The cloud thinned, and Dennis and Gnasher could see down to the jungle again. They heard a rustle and a rumble, and looked down.

Directly below them, the trees were shaking, as if a huge shape was moving through them. For a moment, through a gap, Dennis caught sight of a large black shape. Was that...?

Just then, he heard a faint cry, coming from the other direction.

"Loser!"

Dennis wasn't sure he'd heard it right, at first.

The call came again, slightly louder this time.

"Loooooser!"

Dennis leaned over the rail. "Minnie! Is that you?" he asked the jungle below.

"HA HA HA!" Minnie's voice laughed. "How'd you get up there?"

"Long story," Dennis answered. "So you didn't become dino lunch yet?"

"Not yet! And if anyone does eat me, I'm gonna kung fu them from the inside. Hi-YA!" Minnie replied. "Woah! What's that!? Watch out!"

There was a crashing sound, followed by the

shouting of several large and strong-sounding men and women.

"What's going on?" Dennis shouted down into the jungle below.

"Bit busy," Minnie yelled back. "There's a dinosaur with a crash helmet on down here. Me and the Vikings have got it covered though!"

The cable car had moved over the sound of Minnie's voice by now and was leaving her behind.

"Vikings?" Dennis asked, at the top of his voice.

Minnie was too busy to answer.

Dinosaur with a crash helmet on? wondered Dennis, as the cable car trundled on. It passed under a couple more of the towers that held up the cable before they spotted any more dinosaurs.

It was a Titanosaur. Dennis knew this wasn't the one he'd seen earlier, as its colouring was different. From up here, it didn't look so scary. Its head was now only a little higher than the cable car.

BOOM! BOOM! BOOM! came the

slow thuds of its feet as it strolled lazily through the jungle. It did have a funny face like a dopey dog.

"When you're that big, I guess nothing can hurt you," Dennis said to Gnasher. "This guy's got no worries."

Gnasher had a worry though. He gave Dennis his best "Er, Dennis?" look.

"What's the problem, buddy?"

Dennis looked at the Titanosaur. It was getting nearer, but that was nothing to worry about. At its current speed, it would pass their path long before they...

"Uh-oh."

Dennis had spotted the problem. The Titanosaur was taller than the cable they were dangling from, and it was headed straight for the cable in front of them. It was about to walk right into it.

"Mate, duck!" Dennis shouted as loud as he could.

The animal ahead wasn't smart like the raptors

though. The animal ahead was possibly the world's biggest idiot. It didn't understand any words at all, and two of those words were "mate" and "duck".

"This guy's been wandering around this island for years, and picks today to walk into the wire I'm hanging from!" Dennis exclaimed.

The idiot dinosaur strolled lazily into the cable, which caught under its chin. The cable car jerked up higher, as the cable was pulled taut.

"Urrk!" the Titanosaur choked a little and

137

stuck out its tongue, but kept pushing forwards.

"Argh, the cable's gonna snap!" Dennis cried.

The Titanosaur was starting to get cross with the thing in its way now, but it wasn't getting any smarter so it still didn't duck. The cable was moving too, pulling Dennis and Gnasher closer.

"That's gotta hurt, hasn't it?" Dennis asked Gnasher. "Is it too stupid to feel pain?"

"BLARP!" it shouted.

Dennis clamped his hands over his ears. Gnasher moved his paws over his. The Titanosaur stepped back, a red mark on its neck where the cable had rubbed. The cable car descended a little.

"Finally – it's learning!" shouted Dennis, just before the giant creature bit the cable and began to chew through it.

Back in front of the Mansion, Colonel Grumbly was peering through one of the portholes on the amphibious troop transporter he and Corporal

Clott were hiding inside. From what he could see, it looked like most of the troops had squashed into one of the other transporters, leaving one empty and the one he and Clott were in.

"It looks like the coast is clear," Grumbly said to himself.

"We should play a game while we're waiting to be rescued," Clott said to Grumbly. "Keep our spirits up. I spy, with my little eye..."

"Who are you expecting to rescue us?" Grumbly asked.

Clott thought for a moment. "The army?" he suggested.

"WE ARE THE ARMY!!!"

SCUFFITY-BUMPITY-SCUFF

Luckily, herbivore teeth aren't sharp. So the cable didn't break. Instead, the car slowed as the dinosaur chewed. Its head pulled to one side as the cable tried to keep on moving. In between chomps the cable would jerk forwards until the cable car slammed into the side of the Titanosaur's neck.

As it did so, Dennis was thrown up against the bars and the creature's scaly skin. Gnasher fell between the bars of the cable car and down into the trees below.

"Gnasher!" Dennis screamed as the Titanosaur pushed against the wire again. The cable car was bucking up and down on the cable.

Dennis looked up. The bit of a cable car that grips onto the cable is called the grip. (Must have taken them ages to think of that name!) Dennis didn't know this, but when he looked up he saw that the grip was coming off! This was it. The cable car was either going to hop off the cable entirely, and Dennis would plummet into the dinosaur-infested jungle below, or the cable would snap and the exact same thing would happen.

So Dennis decided to fall out of the cable car on purpose. Well, the plan had actually been to heroically jump towards the bushiest part of a tree below, in the hopes of landing safely – and not too far from Gnasher – but at the last moment the cable car shook again and Dennis's jump ended up as more of a fall.

For a brief moment, all Dennis could see was the side of the Titanosaur's neck whooshing past.

Then – **SCUFFITY-BUMPITY-SCUFF** – he scuffed and bumped along the neck, as it got fatter and wider towards the body.

Finally, Dennis came to a stop.

He'd survived! But the ground was moving... and the neck of the dinosaur was coming up out of the ground...

Dennis realised he wasn't on the ground at all. He turned and saw a dizzy-looking Gnasher, who must have done just as much rolling as him.

"Mate!" he said to his little hairy friend, giving him a hug. "We're still on the dinosaur!"

On its back, to be precise, thought Gnasher.

Dennis looked up to the cable car. It bounced on the cable one more time before falling off it and disappearing into the trees. A second later, there was a terrible crash sound as it hit the ground.

Finally, the stupid Titanosaur figured out how to duck! It stepped back, bent its neck and popped its head under the cable. Trees sailed past as it continued its lazy stroll.

"What a genius!" Dennis said.

With each step, the body beneath them rocked and shook, but there was little danger of falling off. The Titanosaur's back was huge. But now they were headed in the wrong direction.

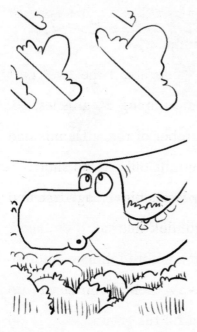

In his diary, Barry Beano had said he was taking the cable car to a place of safety. The Titanosaur they were on, however, was slowly walking them away from the cable. Dennis could see that the cable stretched off towards a large tower in the far distance. The tower had a platform on it. It looked like the end of the line. Safety.

"How do we get off this thing?" Dennis asked Gnasher.

Gnasher gave Dennis his best "I dunno, they don't come with ladders" look.

They decided to go see what was going on at the tail end. (Did I mention it was a big dinosaur?)

Looking at the trees that were scraping past, Dennis had an idea. "We could make it to one of those bigger trees if we jumped."

Gnasher wasn't so sure about the "we" part of that. He was amazing at jumping. Dennis less so. He'd lost count of the number of times Dennis had tried to jump across something only to fall short.

But Dennis had spotted a big enough tree and made up his mind. "That'll do!" he said.

Here we go again, thought Gnasher.

"Ready, steady..." said Dennis, limbering up for the jump.

Gnasher hopped across with ease.

"... Wait for me!" Dennis finished. He leapt across and... well, he missed, didn't he?

"GNASH!"

Dennis was upside down. So things weren't perfect, but at least he'd stopped falling somehow.

He looked up. Gnasher was on a branch above him, holding on to the end of his jumper.

Gnasher gave Dennis his best "I can't hold this much longer!" look.

There was another branch just in front of Dennis, so he swung forwards, grabbed it, and he and Gnasher climbed down.

Dennis smiled for a moment. It felt like they'd achieved something. They'd got down to the ground, safely!

The jungle floor was full of nests.

"This is weird, buddy," Dennis said to Gnasher. "Why are these nests all empty?"

Whatever usually lives here was probably

scared off by the Titanosaur, thought Gnasher. Just then, he saw a feathered thing watching them from a few metres away.

Dennis saw the thing too. He saw another, three or four metres to the side of it. They looked like parrots but three times as big, with little T. rex arms instead of wings. Their feathers were bright yellow with orangey-red tips. And messy. They looked like giants parrots that had been in a fight.

There was a third now. The creatures seemed to appear when Dennis wasn't looking. He'd turn away, then look back, and a battle parrot would be there.

Dennis smiled. "Battle parrot" was a good name for them. The weird, toothy beaks they had looked like they could do some damage.

It was hard to count how many there were now. The battle parrots were all staring at Dennis and Gnasher.

Gnasher slowly backed off, giving Dennis his best "I've got a bad feeling about this" look.

At that same moment, in Beanotown's popular budget supermarket WIDL, Dennis's friend Roger was throwing his head back and groaning loudly.

"Urrrrrgh!" he cried out, as he pushed the trolley for his mum. "We've been in here forever!"

Roger's nickname was Roger the Dodger, because he had the knack of dodging any little chore. This was one of the rare times his parents had tricked him into doing something for them. (Mum had told him they were going to the cinema.)

"We've only been here five minutes!" Roger's mum said.

"It feels like five years," Roger exclaimed. "I'm surprised I don't have a beard!"

Now, you may ask yourself, "Why's that bit in there?"

You'll see, later...

FRYING PAN – FIRE

Dennis and Gnasher were running for their lives, with a hundred battle parrots chasing after them.

"BWALK!" one bwalked, as it hopped and nipped Dennis's arm.

"OW!" Dennis shouted. "That's going to leave a mark!"

"GNASH! GNASH!"

"BWAAAALK!"

It sounded like one of the Hesperonychus to Dennis's left had nipped Gnasher and was regretting it. Dennis couldn't turn to look, though, as he had his own troubles.

"BWALK!"

He thrashed his arms about wildly and batted one away.

"BWALK!" Thwack!

"BWALK!" Thwack!

"BWALK!" THWACK!

"Get off!" Dennis shouted. "Where're all the vegetarians on this stupid island?!"

A Hesperonychus had grabbed hold of his other arm. Dennis glanced to Gnasher, but he was dealing with one hanging from his tail.

Dennis thrashed his arm about, but it stayed on. Trying not to get his fingers caught, he tried to unclamp its jaws.

When he got home this was going to need

some cream. In fact, if he got home, Dennis could probably do with getting in a bath of antiseptic cream!

He noticed that the Hesperonychus's nostrils were at the end of its beaky snout thing. He remembered the hilarious time Dad was asleep on the couch and he'd pinched his nose. After a couple of seconds, Dad had woken with a huge gasp...

Dennis pinched the snout of the creature. Not hard, just so the creature couldn't breathe through its nostrils.

It looked at Dennis crossly.

It's trying to chew my arm off, thought Dennis, but it's cross at me for sticking my fingers in its nose?

Then, just like Dad, the creature gasped for breath – and was forced to let go of Dennis's arm!

There wasn't time to celebrate this small victory, however, as two Hesperonychus had now attached themselves to the back of Dennis's jumper.

Gnasher began to howl like a wolf.

Dennis looked at his faithful friend. Were the dinos hurting him?

They were a bit, but it was only really nips, and Gnasher's tough. He wasn't howling in pain. He was howling like a wolf gathering its pack.

"Hooooowwwwwwwl!" called out Gnasher.

The Hespys on his tail let go, as did one of the ones on Dennis's jumper.

"HOOOOOOWWWWWWWWL!"

The other Hespy let go of Dennis too.

Dennis and Gnasher stopped running. They were surrounded, and out of breath, but the creatures seemed unsure what to do.

"What's going on?" Dennis asked Gnasher.

Let's rewind.

You remember when Dennis and Gnasher had escaped the raptors, in the lift?

They didn't like that. They sniffed around, only for Fletcher to see Dennis leaving the building in some sort of contraption hanging from a wire.

So the raptors decided to follow Dennis, in the jungle below. This had led them near some tasty-looking Vikings, but the three raptors would have been outnumbered so stayed hidden.

As the raptors had followed Dennis, though, a dread feeling had come over them all, one by one. It was the feeling that they too were being followed.

Eventually they caught up with Dennis and Gnasher, but the Titanosaur stopped their progress. The falling cable car almost landed on poor Clarence!

From a distance, they watched as Dennis and Gnasher came down from the Titanosaur and blundered into the Hesperonychus nests. At last, it seemed they would be able to catch up with Dennis.

Now our two stories join...

Gnasher howled again and a raptor jumped into the middle of the Hespys and clamped its jaws onto one.

"BWALK!" it cried, as the raptor quickly picked it up and with a jerk of his neck threw it away. The rest of the little animals darted off into the jungle.

"Bleurgh!" Fletcher the raptor said. "I do so hate Hesperonychus. It's the feathers!"

The three raptors looked pretty much identical. It was only possible to tell which one was Fletcher when they spoke.

"Hesperonychus," Dennis said, clicking his fingers. "I was trying to remember what they're called!"

(There was only one subject Dennis was prepared to learn about and that was dinosaurs... and skateboard tricks. Okay, that's two things.)

"Knew I'd seen them somewhere before." Dennis smiled broadly, with his fists on his hips in triumph.

Then he realised he'd been talking to a raptor. The smile quickly melted. Dennis looked over his shoulder. Two more were behind him.

This didn't seem right at all. You don't get

saved from a bad thing, by a thing that's even worse! That's like a snake wrapping itself around you, then it getting scared off by an alligator.

"I thought the Gnashersaurus had got you," Dennis said.

"We decided to take the stairs," said one of the raptors behind Dennis. "Rather than hang around to get eaten."

(Luckily for the raptors, the door to the stairs was a small, single door, through which the Gnashersaurus rex could not fit.)

The raptor in front of Dennis – Fletcher, the leader – had done most of the talking back in the kitchen. Now it was Dennis's turn.

"We're not your enemies," Dennis explained. "We're on your side. I want to protect the island as much as you!"

"You're human," the third raptor said, a female. "It's not your job to help us. Your job is to run and scream."

She smiled. It wasn't one of those smiles that makes you relax.

"Adeline's right, old bean," Fletcher said to Dennis. "Humans have a bad track record."

Although today's humans were the first humans these raptors had actually met, they'd heard stories passed down from their great-grandparents.

As Fletcher took a step towards them, Gnasher howled again. It seemed like a neverending howl.

"Hooooooooooow wwwwwwwwl!"

"Why is he doing that?" Clarence asked. "It sounds like—"

"HOOOOO OOOOOWWW WWWWWL!!!"

The second howl wasn't Gnasher.

The Gnashersaurus rex was only a few metres away, sort of behind Fletcher. It let out its best and most terrifying roar.

"ROAR!!!"

"Is this thing here to help us or eat us?" Dennis asked Gnasher.

Gnasher gave Dennis his best "I have no idea!" look.

Fletcher ran straight for Dennis. Dennis shut his eyes and braced himself, but he felt the raptor run past.

The roar finished, and Dennis carefully opened one eye.

The raptors had gone!

"So..." Dennis started. "The raptors saved us from the Hesperonychus, and the Gnashersaurus saved us from the raptors... Who saves us from the Gnashersaurus?"

The Gnashersaurus trudged over to Gnasher

and sniffed him. Then licked him.

Naturally, the Gnashersaurus rex thought Gnasher was a baby one of him.

Phew! thought Gnasher. At least he was off the imaginary dinner table, but what about Dennis?

The Gnashersaurus rex took a step towards Dennis, a growl starting to rumble up his throat.

Gnasher pondered over the problem as he licked at a patch of barbecue sauce on Dennis's arm that he had missed earlier.

The Gnashersaurus rex stopped in his tracks. Licking was the international animal sign for "I like you." Even he knew that. And if the baby T. rex liked this human then perhaps he wasn't too much of a threat after all.

He took another step towards Dennis who cringed but made no move to run. Lowering his nostrils to within inches of Dennis's face, the Gnashersaurus rex sniffed deeply then reached out with his long tongue and gave Dennis, one big, slobbery lick.

Hmmm, he thought. Was that the leftover taste of barbecue sauce?

The two troop transporters slowly made their way through the jungle. One was overcrowded with highly trained soldiers. The other had only Corporal Clott and Colonel Grumbly on board.

"I spy, with my little eye," Clott began, as the transporter rolled past a giant Venus flytrap plant. "Something beginning with... that weird, hungry-looking plant with teeth!"

Grumbly gripped the steering wheel tighter. He was totally lost, and Clott was making life unbearable.

"That's not how you play the game!" he shouted.

"But I spied a big, hungry plant with teeth,"

Clott pointed out. "Now you've got to guess what it is."

"ARRRGH!" Grumbly yelled. "You've said what it is! You've just told me it's a plant!"

"Well done, your lordship," Clott said. "Your turn!"

Grumbly slammed the brakes on and turned round in his seat. "If you don't shut up, you're walking home!" he warned him.

Clott looked out of the porthole he was sat next to. An enormous eye, the size of a dinner plate, looked back.

Clott decided shutting up might be for the best.

THE THING IN THE SACK

Earlier – sometime after Dennis and the others had arrived on Duck Island, but before Dennis fell from the cable car – Einar the Viking was hunting alone. He had his spear in hand, an axe tucked in his belt and a sack in his other hand. He intended to fill the sack with his daily catch.

Creeping though the undergrowth, Einar spied movement through the foliage. Relatively small movement. Not the kind of huge movement that had a habit of belonging to one of the larger, hungrier, wingless dragons.

Creeping nearer, Einar saw that it was a human! A human who was not a Viking. Presumably the bad sort of human he'd heard stories of from the elders.

Had they returned to the land? He decided it would be best to stuff this person in his sack and take them back to the ship, which was parked nearby.

Haabjorn would probably want to know what this invader wanted.

So Einar jumped from the bushes and threw the sack over the newcomer, before they could even turn round.

Boy did that sack fight!

It was like the sack had nine angry wolves in it and all those wolves had boxing gloves on and had been taught how to fight.

Einar tied the sack shut and was forced to drag it along the ground, after a few attempts at carrying it ended with either being kicked or punched. Or both.

Those poor, poor Vikings. They never stood a chance.

A few minutes later, Einar dragged the sack into the clearing in which the ship was parked. The previously angry sack was now quite still.

"What's that you got there?" one of the others asked.

Before Einar could answer, the sack jumped up and dived towards the voice it had just heard. The Vikings all backed away from the furious sack, as a girl burst from it, growling and snarling.

Minnie saw the cowering Vikings and shouted, **"COME ON THEN! I'LL BITE YOUR BEARDS OFF!!!"**

It was then they saw it – Einar too, as he'd only seen her from behind. Minnie bore a striking resemblance to Grunhilda the Grumpy!

Before Minnie or the Vikings could say anything else, a strange twinkly music came from nowhere, and everything started to go a bit wibbly wobbly.

"ARRRRGH! What's happening?" Haabjorn asked.

"IT'S A FLASHBACK!" Minnie shouted over the increasingly loud twinkly music. **"HOLD ONTO YOUR BUTT..."**

It was the year 815. A Tuesday. A small band of brave Vikings were on their way to England. Just to do a little raid. Perhaps pinch some sheep. Steal some gold, and maybe get an ice cream.

Their leader was Dagfinn – a handsome, brave warrior, with an even handsomer, braver beard.

Dagfinn liked a good raid. Raiding was his favourite hobby. But this time, before they reached shore, they were caught in a terrible storm, the likes of which they'd never seen. The waves grew and grew, taller than any wave Dagfinn had ever even heard of.

The sea rose up in front of them. The powerful wind was blowing the sailing ship up and up the ever steeper water that now towered above them. The sea became steeper and steeper still, until the wave was a wall of water.

Dagfinn and his shipmates held on as tightly as they could. The ship was now pointing straight up!

Roaring, the wave crashed into what would one day be Beanotown.

Dagfinn woke, battered and bruised, with Grunhilda the Grumpy standing over him, waving an axe around her head. The axe was far too big for her, and she was screaming and shouting angrily.

He sat up.

Grunhilda was waving her axe at a... a... dragon!?!

Dagfinn had never seen such a creature with his own eyes. They were beasts of legend.

The dragon snarled, and snapped angrily, but brave Grunhilda fended it off.

Around Dagfinn, the other Vikings also began to wake, amongst the wreckage of their ship. Seeing the wingless dragon before them, they quickly took up swords. In response, the Lythronax (for that's what it really was) thought, Aw, forget this! and went back into the jungle.

The wave had crashed their ship down onto Duck Island. And it was there they stayed.

There was more to the flashback. There was going to be a montage about Grunhilda growing into a powerful warrior queen, and a picture of her being painted on a cave wall somewhere, which is how the Vikings now thought they recognised Minnie. Instead Minnie burst the flashback with a, **"Grrrrrah! Get off! Go on! Shoo! Stupid flashback!"**

"It's Grunhilda the Grumpy! She's returned from Valhalla!"

Minnie had seen the movies. Valhalla was some sort of Viking afterlife-type place that only great warriors could get into.

Grunhilda the Grumpy must have been an awesome warrior.

"THAT'S RIGHT!" she shouted, **"WHO WANTS A BOP ON THE NOGGIN?!"**

A few minutes later, Minnie was getting some

sort of royal tour of a Viking longboat that was on wheels in the middle of the jungle. The Vikings proudly showed Minnie the foot pedals that made the wheels turn and nervously invited her back to their village.

"Yeah, sure!" Minnie readily agreed. She then hopped back, into her best kung fu pose, as two Allosauruses trotted up to the land-ship.

Haabjorn and Einar held Minnie back, and proudly explained that they'd tamed many "dragons".

So it came to be that, moments later, Minnie was crashing through the jungle on a Viking land-boat, tooting a horn, followed by two eight-metre-long Allosauruses.

She was too busy having fun to notice that they'd crashed past a steam train with Walter and Wilbur on board.

It wasn't that long after that when Minnie did notice something, though. Up through a gap in the trees, she saw Dennis in a cable car!

"Loser!" Minnie called up to him.

No reply. Had he heard? She tried again, louder this time: "Loooooser!"

She'd taunted him for a bit longer, before spotting a Pachycephalosaurus that was heading straight for them. (Pachycephalosaurus is the one with the super thick skull, for head butting.)

The Pachycephalosaurus crashed into the boat and put quite a nasty hole in it. (The boat actually had quite a few holes in it... well, I say a few. Loads. Thankfully, if your boat is on land it doesn't sink.)

The Vikings attacked, shouting various battle cries. Normally if lots of humans attacked an animal, you'd say it was cruel. It's certainly not something I'd include in a book. But it was clear from the start that the Vikings were the ones in trouble.

In seconds, five Vikings were on their butts, surrounded by their smashed-up shields.

"What's going on?" Dennis had shouted down to them.

"Bit busy!" Minnie shouted back. "There's a dinosaur with a crash helmet on down here. Me and the Vikings have got it covered though!"

Minnie and the Vikings had nothing covered.

Minnie jumped off the back of the boat and landed on one of the tame Allosauruses. Being half the size of an Allosaurus, the Pachycephalosaurus ran away.

The Allosauruses chased it, Minnie still riding on one of them.

STOP GOING ON ABOUT HELEN

Dennis didn't know what to do.

He was deep in the jungle, with Gnasher and the Gnashersaurus rex, and he didn't have a plan.

The original plan had been clear: save the dinosaurs from the Mayor's money-making scheme.

It wasn't a good plan. It hadn't really been worked out properly. Plan A got binned as soon as they got to the island and it became obvious that dinosaurs don't need help.

Plan B quickly became don't get eaten – an even simpler plan.

Now Dennis was safe, he didn't know what to do. Should he go back to plan A? Stop the Mayor? Did the Mayor still have to be stopped? He'd probably been lunch for something by now.

I could go home and get my dinner, he thought to himself. Or ride a dinosaur.

Elsewhere, the Mayor and his son's train journey was approaching its end.

They had hoped that the train would take them close to the edge of the island. It hadn't. It had taken them round and round and up and up a mountain.

"Where's Helen when you need her?" the Mayor asked.

"Stop going on about Helen," Walter complained. "What about me?"

"You'll make me tea?" the Mayor asked.

"Of course not! **Make your own tea!**" Walter thought silently to himself.

It was then, without doing anything, that Helen made it to Walter's revenge list.

Thoughts of revenge quickly gave way to thoughts of panic when the end of the track loomed ahead. It looked like there was a small station there.

"How do you stop this thing?" Walter shouted at his father.

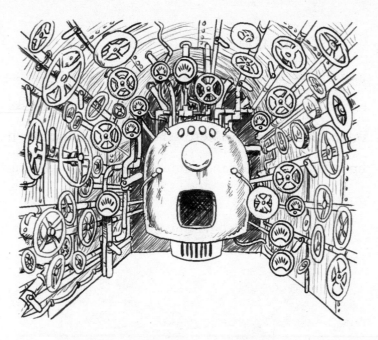

"How should I know?!" the Mayor shouted back. "I'm a mayor!"

It was only now that they realised they hadn't done much to start the train.

The controls must have been set on "go" before the fire in the boiler had been lit. Wilbur had managed to light the coal, and the machine had started to chuff along on its own. Now it was getting important that the controls be set to "stop", but the controls were... well, look at them!

CLANG!

The train smashed into the buffers at the end of the track, and went over them with an incredible bump. Walter and Wilbur were thrown up to the ceiling.

The train carried on, through the small station. It smashed through the ticket stalls, before ending up in a muddy patch at the side of the station, where the wheels chuffed round and round in the mud.

Walter and Wilbur staggered out. There were only two paths open to them: walk back the way they came, along the train track, or up the few remaining stairs to the mountain top.

From the top of the stairs, they could see that the mountain itself was rather unimpressive. It was more like a tall hill, but it did give a good view of the island. From where they were, Walter and Wilbur could see all of the jungle and it looked peaceful enough. But every now and again one of the well-camouflaged Titanosaurs would move. This reminded Walter and Wilbur that deeper in the trees and bushes there were predators...

Walter turned round. He noticed that the top of the mountain was quite flat.

It was in fact an extinct volcano. At some

point in the past, hot lava had bubbled up inside the volcano, filling it up to the brim. Then, instead of blowing, the volcano had calmed down. The lava filling it cooled and turned to rock, and for the next few million years it stayed like that.

It was hard to tell if the building on top of the volcano had fallen down a hundred years ago or if, a hundred years ago, its building had been interrupted. The uneven walls stood only waist-high in most places. In the middle of this half-done or half-undone building there was a large and strange-looking object.

It was a large rock, bigger than a beach ball, with a deep crack running down the middle. Holding this rock together was an odd device. It was a kind of framework, holding lots of clamps that looked to be pushing the rock together.

Walter walked up to the asteroid and touched it. Amazing and exciting to think that it had once crashed into the Earth with such power.

There are 10 Titanosaurs here. Can you find them all?

There was nothing about this contraption that seemed obviously dangerous to Walter, but it made him feel afraid all the same.

"Leave that alone!" Dennis shouted.

Walter and Wilbur looked around. Dennis was poking his head up over on the far side of the mountain's flat top.

"Or you'll what?!" asked Walter.

Dennis rose up higher and higher, until his body was visible over the edge of the ex-volcano. He rose higher and higher still, as the Gnashersaurus he and Gnasher were riding finished its climb.

"Or I'll 'dinosaur' you!" Dennis answered.

"Got yourself a dinosaur, have you?" came the reply.

Wilbur, Walter, Dennis, Gnasher and the Gnashersaurus all turned to see Minnie as she rose and rose from the other side of the ex-volcano. She was riding on the back of an Allosaurus, followed by another Allosaurus.

"I've got two!" she beamed.

Dennis was cross with Minnie, but he tried not to show it. When you turn up somewhere on the back of a dinosaur, everyone's meant to be all, like, **"WOW**! You're on a dinosaur!" not, "Only got the one dinosaur have you?"

Partly to draw attention away from this, he shouted: "Leave that asteroid alone! "That rock is what's keeping the island small. Break that, and everything will grow huge and spread across Beanotown!"

"Oh right! Thank you," the Mayor said. "Better

leave it alone then, son. Good idea, Dennis."

Wilbur found the town hard enough to control without dinosaurs.

Dennis didn't know what to say. Things weren't meant to be this easy.

He'd just gone on a random stroll on his new dinosaur, and he'd spotted Walter and Wilbur's train choo-chooing up a little mountain. It had just gone out of view when he'd heard a crash. So, naturally, he'd come to investigate.

The Vikings that had been trying to keep up with Minnie failed to do so. She was too fast. She had closed in on the bony-headed dinosaur she was chasing, then had spotted Dennis in the distance on a dinosaur of his own. She'd decided to show off the fact that she had two, and had followed him up here.

Now, everyone was together for the final, epic showdown... and the big boss had just agreed with Dennis and said, "Good idea!"

Imagine that happening in other stories. Harry Potter faces Voldemort and says, "Stop being evil." Voldemort replies, "Okay. Good idea," and stops being evil. The end.

Or James Bond finally gets to the evil genius who's been trying to take over the world. He says, "Stop trying to take over the world!" and the bad guy says, "Yes. Okay." The end.

Not exciting, I know, but that's what happened.

"Oh," said Dennis, "Okay."

THE END...

What are you still reading for?

That's it. That's how the story ended.

Bit of a lame ending, this one, if you ask me. The start was quite good, and once they got on Duck Island things got really exciting. Remember the talking raptors? Shame we didn't see them one last time...

Thinking about it, I should probably have written about the time Minnie ended up fighting evil aliens in space, or when Dennis ended up 70 years in the past and went to school with Gran.

Or a third example I can't think of at the moment.

Thinking about it more, though, there was other stuff that happened after Wilbur agreed with Dennis that the asteroid should be left alone. And it all happened right after that moment...

BECAUSE

"GET AWAY FROM WHATEVER THAT IS!" shouted Dennis at Walter, who was standing in front of what looked like a giant boiler near the asteroid. The various tubes coming out of it connected to the clamps that were holding the asteroid together.

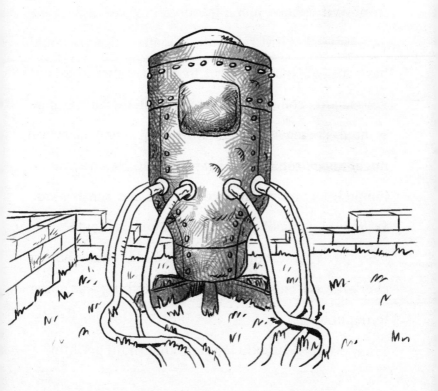

Walter pulled a tube out. There was a loud hiss, as air escaped the hose. The asteroid moved slightly.

"What are you doing?!" Dennis and Wilbur both said together.

Walter smiled a wicked smile and pulled out another hose. There was another hiss and the asteroid moved a little more. The crack down the front of it opened just a fraction.

"GET HIM!" Minnie shouted. Dennis could have got the Gnashersaurus to swipe Walter away but it was hard enough to just get it to go in the direction he wanted. There was also the worry that a dino tail swipe might knock some more hoses out too. He and Minnie jumped down from their dinosaurs and ran towards Walter, who quickly pulled two more hoses out.

The asteroid fell open, and immediately everyone started feeling tingly. Something was going to happen!

"Why?" asked Dennis. What did it get him?

The why was easy. Walter broke the asteroid apart mainly because Dennis wanted it not to happen.

Also, Walter was aware he was in the middle of a dinosaur island. There had been little chance of him getting off the island safely. But if the dinosaurs were spread out across Beanotown, Walter had more chance of escaping, because there'd be other people for the dinosaurs to chew in Beanotown.

Yes, he was putting everyone in Beanotown in

great danger, but in doing so he was in less danger. So it was worth it.

Walter didn't say any of this though.

He just said, "Because."

Without the asteroid keeping everything on the island small, everything on the island became big. But not at the same time or the same speed. The effect was... lumpy, in much the same way as popcorn in a pan doesn't all pop at the same time.

Walter himself was one of the first things to "pop" back to normal size. Dennis grabbed Walter's jumper, to pull him away from the boiler thing. As he did so, Walter quickly grew, until he towered over Dennis, who was still hanging on, mid-air.

Gnasher grew next. Quick as a shot, he ballooned to the same size as the Gnashersaurus rex. Then, all around them, random things grew at random speeds.

Looking out across the jungle, Dennis saw that the effect was spreading across the island. Trees were bursting up and up. Suddenly, it was as if many of these things were shrinking again. They weren't. Dennis was getting bigger!

Colonel Grumbly's grip on the wheel relaxed. This was looking familiar. That rock, that tree stump... Yes, they'd come this way this morning. They were close to the edge of the island!

This moment of happiness was quickly burst, however, by a rumbling sound. There was something behind them. The transporter was starting to shake too.

Grumbly stood on his chair, opened the hatch above his head and looked back.

Then wished he hadn't.

Imagine shaking out a bed sheet or duvet. As you shake the cloth, a kind of ripple or wave passes down the sheet. Now imagine you're a little bug on that sheet, as it's shaken from the other end.

From your point of view, the Earth itself is lifting up in front of you, and it's headed your way! Now imagine that instead of a duvet it's a jungle. Try to picture a tidal wave of greenery headed towards you, and behind that wave, impossible things. Creatures and trees growing at impossible speeds, into impossible sizes.

Colonel Grumbly ducked back inside and shut the hatch tight, as the ripple hit.

Meanwhile Boat Rental Guy wasn't happy. Number four boat had sprung a leak somewhere.

Next to the boat, he noticed a tiny wave come into shore. This may have only been a tiny wave, but Boat Rental Guy still thought it was weird. Duck ponds don't have waves.

A larger wave came to shore. There were more, and they were coming from the island.

BRG frowned. It was none of his business – the Mayor had told him that. "It's none of your business!" he'd said, when BRG asked why so much of the army was trying to squeeze onto such a tiny island.

A couple more waves came from the island as...

"BLARP!"

The rest of Boat Rental Guy's thoughts were blown away by the incredible noise. It sounded like all the trumpets in the world, parping together.

A strange head on an impossibly long neck rose up out of the middle of the island, and continued to grow up into the sky! Strange plants and bushes tumbled and fell out of the island. Rocks tumbled out too. Rocks so big they couldn't possibly have been on the island in the first place!

The island seemed to be expanding, unrolling and inflating, like an emergency life raft.

BOOM!

The Titanosaurus stepped out of the growing chaos, as something much smaller ran out into the park. It looked like a toy raptor?

The ground rippled as roots and vines from the island spilled out, and the raptor fell on its side. It began to grow. By the time it was back on its feet, a second later, BRG could see that it wasn't a raptor at all. It was a fully grown T. rex!

BOOM! The Titanosaurus took another step.

The jungle trees and bushes quickly grew and expanded past Boat Rental Guy. Before he knew it, it didn't feel like he was in the park anymore. It was a jungle. He dived into number four boat, as roots and vines grew and wriggled underneath it, pushing it away from the shore.

"What's happening?" the Viking next to BRG asked.

A Viking?!

Then suddenly the Viking was lost again in the tumbling, expanding greenery.

A family of Triceratopses thundered past.

"I'm not cleaning all this up!" BRG said to himself, as one of the army transporters he'd seen rlier tumbled past. The jungle wriggled and expanded across the park. Anything fixed down stayed where it was, as the jungle worked round it. But anything not fixed down was picked up and carried along on the leafy, dinosaur-infested wave.

BUTTON IT, KID!

When we last saw Dennis's mate Will, he was finishing a cup of tea, having watched Dennis, Minnie and Gnasher climb the tree in his back garden to get into the army base. Shortly after that, he decided to get properly dressed and go out.

Somehow he drifted to the park and before long found himself on the slide. It was one of those metal curly tubes you often see in parks. Will slid down it. Down and around he slid in darkness, emerging at the bottom... into a jungle?!

The timing had been perfect. In the short time Will was in the slide, the jungle had rolled out all around it. So as he reached the bottom, he thought what anybody else would have thought.

This slide must be a portal to the Amazon!

Then Will noticed that the swings were still there. And on one of the swings was a raptor.

The raptor smiled at him.

"These are fun," it said.

"I guess I'm not in Beanotown anymore," thought Will.

Corporal Clott and Colonel Grumbly felt like they were inside a tumble dryer, as the transporter rolled over and over. For a moment, while they tumbled over and over, it seemed to Colonel Grumbly that Clott was bigger somehow, but quickly he seemed to go back to normal size.

Eventually the transporter stopped. Thankfully, it was the right way up. Grumbly got up and looked out of the window.

"Beans, three for two?" he said.

"Beans, three for two?" Clott asked.

They stepped out into WIDL car park. Grumbly blinked at the poster in its window: Beans, three for two. A really reasonable deal.

"Beans, three for two!" Grumbly answered. "How are we in WIDL car park?"

Dennis's friend Roger and Roger's mum were exiting the popular discount supermarket. The trolley Roger was pushing soon jammed up on the roots that now snaked across the car park.

While they'd been shopping, it seemed, a jungle had grown up around them.

"How long were we in there?" Roger asked. "'Quick shop', you said, Mum! Civilisation has collapsed and Nature's reclaimed the Earth!"

Roger's mum was confused. There was a

new guy on the till and he'd been pretty slow, but it hadn't been quite that long, surely?

Teacher was standing alone on the Beanotown underground platform. He looked at his watch. The train was late.

He heard a rumble. Teacher looked down the platform into the tunnel. The rumble got louder. It was too loud for a train.

Sounding like an avalanche, the rumble quickly passed by, above him. It was on the surface, up on street level.

In the following quiet, he heard a tap, tap, tap nearby. Someone wearing high heels was approaching.

Teacher looked back up the platform to where the sound was coming from.

Tap, tap, tap...

A raptor stepped out onto the platform. Its long claws were tap, tap, tapping on the tiles as it

walked. The creature looked up the platform in the other direction.

Teacher stepped back towards the passage through to the southbound platform, but the raptor turned and saw him.

Teacher screamed, and ran through to the other platform.

The rumble started again. No, it was different this time. This was definitely a train!

Teacher ran out onto the southbound platform and jumped on the train as it arrived.

The doors to the train hadn't closed yet when the raptor calmly walked through onto the southbound platform.

WHOOSH! The doors closed and the train set off.

"PHEW!" said Teacher, slumping down onto a seat.

"That looked like a raptor!" one of the other passengers commented.

"I blame global warming," said another.

In Beanotown cinema, everyone was just settling down to the latest blockbuster dinosaur movie.

"I don't see the point in 3D!" one of the grumpy viewers said, unfolding his arms to wave them at the screen. He was cross at having to pay more. "Real life's 3D! When I'm walking around the streets it's all in 3D and I'm not all, like, 'Oooh!

Look at all the 3D!' I'm just like, 'Meh, street!' The effects are never all that."

A Stegosaurus crashed through the doors behind them, so tall it smashed out the wall above the door with its back plates. The beast sauntered down the aisle past them and ripped through the screen.

"Okay... That was alright, I guess," he admitted.

Minnie the Minx ended up in Beanotown's swimming pool.

As she'd tumbled along – and grown and grown, back to normal size – a tree had been just in front of her. When they'd reached the pool, it had smashed through the floor-to-ceiling windows, leaving a huge hole for her to fall through. The tree was in the pool with her now, as was the Allosaurus she had been riding.

The Allosaurus gave her its best "What just happened?" look, then glanced around for his brother. But its brother wasn't there – he must have been lost somewhere, in the confusion.

In the pool next to Minnie and the tree and

the Allosaurus stood a mum holding her toddler. The mum's mouth was wide open. The toddler looked worried. Its bottom lip wobbled. He was about to burst out crying.

"Button it, kid!" Minnie ordered the toddler.

The Mayor washed up on the steps of the town hall.

What had just happened had been strange. He'd been on Duck Island, on the top of the mountain, with his son and those other children. Walter had unplugged the thing holding the asteroid together... then things got odd.

Everything around Wilbur had begun to change size. The ground under him had shook and, even though he'd thought he was far from the edge, somehow he'd fallen over it.

The Mayor had tumbled down the mountain, past the train and train station, which looked like toys. Then there'd been nothing but leaves and branches and grass and bugs, tumbling over and over, and all along the feeling that he was moving.

Now, on the steps of the town hall, Wilbur could see the train again. It was leaning up against the bank, normal-sized.

The door behind the Mayor opened. Helen had a cup of tea in her hand.

Wilbur looked up hopefully.

"BLARP!"

Helen looked up to see a Titanosaur towering over the buildings in the town centre.

"D-d-d-d-dinos-s-s," Helen stammered.

"Yes," said the Mayor. "Dinosaurs. Try to keep up, Helen. There's a good girl. Shall we go in and have some tea?"

AD-O-BLOB!

Dennis and Gnasher ended up by someone's front door. The Gnashersaurus rex was nowhere to be seen.

Gnasher was sat on Dennis's lap. He gave Dennis his best "That was interesting" look.

Gran opened the door, and Dennis fell back into the hall. She looked at the impenetrable jungle all around.

"Garden's getting a bit overgrown," she said. "I'll give you 50 pence to mow the grass and prune the hedge."

Dennis rolled his eyes.

"Gran, it's not whenever you're from," he told her. "You can't buy a car for a quid anymore!"

A Pterodactyl landed in a nearby tree that, until recently, hadn't been there.

Gran frowned. "What did you do?" she asked.

"It wasn't me!" Dennis complained, as his

phone started ringing. "When something happens, why does everyone think it was me?"

The phone continued to ring.

"Because of everything you've done in your life so far," Gran answered. "Are you going to answer that?"

Dennis answered it.

"This jungle full of dinosaurs better not be anything to do with you!" Mum shouted down the phone. "Also... **dinner!!!**"

"I'll be round in five minutes," Dennis grumbled.

"What's the one that looks like a duck?" Dad asked later, as he held Dennis's baby sister, and Dennis ate his dinner.

"Hadrosaur," said Dennis, with a face full of cold mash potato.

"I've just seen a Hadrosaur!" Dad said proudly. "Are they carnivores?"

"Don't think so," Dennis answered.

"Can you say Hadrosaur?" Dad asked baby Bea. "Had-ro-saur."

"Ad-o-blob!" Bea answered.

"Clever girl!" said Dad.

Mum was standing next to Dennis, looming over him. She was doing her best looming, with her fists on her hips and everything.

"Are you going to do something about all this?!" she shout-asked.

Throwing Gnasher one of his sausages, Dennis answered, "I told you, I didn't do it!"

Dennis kind of liked the new jungle-covered, dinosaur-infested, town. He thought it was cool. Yes, there was now a small chance of getting eaten on the way to school, and that small chance was actually quite large, but it didn't stop it being cool.

"You've got a baby sister!"

"So?" asked Dennis.

"So, your baby sister isn't growing up in a town full of dinosaurs!" Mum informed Dennis.

"What's the one with bony triangles on its back?" Dad asked, looking out of the window.

"Stegosaurus," Dennis replied.

"Ste-go-saur-us!" Dad said to Bea.

"Stop that!" Mum told Dad.

"She's going to have to know her dinosaur names if she's going to grow up in a town full of dinosaurs," Dad answered.

"Steg-og-blob!" Bea said.

"She's not growing up in Dinotown!" Mum

insisted. "Dennis is going to put everything back as it was. Or no Wi-Fi!"

"What?!" Dennis and Dad said together. Dad had invented the "No Wi-Fi" punishment, but immediately regretted it, as turning off the Wi-Fi meant he had no Wi-Fi either so he couldn't watch the football.

"Why am I getting punished for something I didn't do?" Dennis complained.

"Because I don't want to live in a dinosaur park!" said Mum.

After pudding, Dennis stormed out of the house. (Gnasher sort of trotted out. He wasn't bothered about Wi-Fi.)

It was typical Mum. She could suck the fun out of anything. Dennis had wanted a flamethrower for Christmas and somehow she'd got to Santa and stopped that happening. The chainsaw he'd asked for for his birthday also hadn't shown up.

He'd tried to stop all of this from happening.

Tried and failed. To Dennis's mind it was a done deal now and the best thing to do was accept it. Like that time he spilt ink all over the living room carpet. There was no fixing that!

Still, knowing Walter and the Mayor there'd be some more evil on the way. The Mayor would maybe train the raptors to be his personal raptor army, or Walter would get something like a T. rex as a pet to help him bully everyone or something. Dennis thought. Maybe there was a way to mend the asteroid and return the dinosaurs to mini-size? Then everything could go back to normal.

Just then an idea occurred to him. It was time to pay Gran another visit. There was something of hers he was going to need...

As Dennis rounded the corner at the end of Gran's street, the borrowed item safely stowed in his pocket, a T. rex roared at him.

"ROOOOOOOOOAR!!!"

"Cool!" Dennis replied. "I was hoping to bump into you. You've still got it going on, big guy!"

"Gnash! Gnash!" added Gnasher, in a friendly way.

The T. rex was slightly confused by this reaction. Normally the creature she'd roared at would run away. There'd then be a fun little chase, followed by dinner.

"GNASH!"

The T. rex turned to see the slightly larger Gnashersaurus rex behind her. Oh...

While the T. rex ran off, Dennis held his arms open wide at the Gnashersaurus. As best he could, he hid his worry that it might not remember him (and would eat him instead).

"Mate! What happened to you?" he asked the huge dinosaur that wasn't able to answer.

Even if it could talk, it wouldn't remember what had happened to it. The Gnashersaurus remembered Dennis and Gnasher's smell though,

and that smell was in the "friends" bit of its tiny brain. So that was enough.

Dennis and Gnasher jumped up onto the Gnashersaurus's back.

"Take us to the asteroid, mate!" Dennis asked.

But the Gnashersaurus didn't understand any of those words.

"Gnash!" Gnasher gnashed.

"Gnash?" the Gnashersaurus asked.

"Gnash! Gnash!" Gnasher answered.

"Gnash, gnash, gnash?" Gnashersaurus asked.

"Gnash, gnash, gnash, gnash, gnash, gnash!" Gnasher replied.

They both had a big laugh about that, because of what a funny joke it was.

The Gnashersaurus sniffed the air. There were a lot of confusing smells around, but he thought he smelled something familiar, and set off.

The Allosaurus Minnie was riding was whining like a sad puppy. Minnie guessed that he missed his buddy.

"There, there, big guy," she said, stroking the back of the Allosaurus's neck. "We'll find him."

Meanwhile, Walter was scrabbling through the undergrowth. Going off the shop signs he could see through the thick jungle, he was most likely on Beanotown's main shopping street. That meant he was quite far from home, but the town hall was —

His train of thought stopped abruptly, when he came face to face with a raptor.

"Hello," said Fletcher, in his posh voice. "This is a bit of a to-do, isn't it?"

Walter noticed there was another raptor behind him. Then a third arrived.

"You don't want to eat me," Walter pleaded. "I'm bony and made out of poison!"

"That's what dinner usually says," said the raptor behind him. "Or growls to that effect."

"You're all cold-hearted evil-doers only out for yourselves!" Walter blurted out.

"Ye-es. Your point being?" asked Fletcher.

"My point being, you're like me!" Walter continued. "Do you like this?" he asked the raptors, waving his arms around.

The raptors looked around at all the juicy humans stumbling through the newly arrived jungle.

"Yes," said Fletcher. "Very much so."

If the raptors had said they didn't like it, Walter was going to help them repair the asteroid and shrink everything back to normal. But seeing as they'd said the opposite, he said...

"Well, I made it happen! And if I know my arch-enemy Dennis like I think I know Dennis," Walter continued, "he's currently trying to save the town! He's always saving this or that. He won't let me destroy anything!"

"This Dennis fellow," Fletcher asked. "He doesn't have untidy hair and a red-and-black striped jumper, does he?"

"That's him!" Walter said. "Do you know him?"

"Oh we know him. In fact, I find him slightly more annoying than you," said the raptor called Adeline, from behind Walter. "And we know his friend too."

"Minnie?" Walter asked.

"No, not unless Minnie is 20 feet tall and covered in hair and teeth," Fletcher replied. "We can't do this alone. We need Mr Serious."

"Mr... Serious?" Walter asked.

MR SERIOUS LOOKED EXTREMELY SERIOUS

The asteroid was exactly where it had been, at the exact centre of Duck Island. When everything on the island had expanded across Beanotown, it had expanded away from the asteroid, like the ripple from a pebble.

In fact, the asteroid was the only thing still where it had been, up a small hill-like mountain, where the park used to be. Lots of bits and pieces from the park littered its slopes, as the little ex-volcano had grown and expanded under them. The swings, for example, were now halfway up the mountain. Next to them was the slide that Will was still hiding inside.

Dennis, Gnasher and the Gnashersaurus had reached the fence that used to circle the park but now circled Mount Duck.

"Okay," Dennis said to his buddies, as he and

Gnasher jumped down off the Gnashersaurus. "All we gotta do is get up there and squash the two bits of weird rock back together, and everything goes back to normal. Easy!"

This was obviously easier said than done. Everything, everywhere was... messy. The entire town was now in a similar state, mess-wise, to Dennis's bedroom. As Dennis knew, his room was impossible to get across without stepping on and breaking some toy or other. Only these weren't toys.

As the mountain had expanded, it had grown up underneath the cars parked nearby. A number of these were now perched unsteadily on its rather steep slopes, close to tipping point.

Dennis took a step forwards, and one of the cars tipped and rolled and crashed and bashed towards them. He moved to dodge out of the way, but tripped on a vine and fell.

The car just missed him.

Dennis looked up the hill. Having dived out of the way, he was now in the path of a different car, if that chose to tumble down. He looked at the Gnashersaurus.

"Like I said – easy!"

Some distance away, slurping the last of his tea, the Mayor was watching Dennis through the telescope he used to spy on everyone in town. At this distance he couldn't make out what was being said, but he had seen him narrowly avoid the tumbling car.

Wilbur rightly assumed Dennis was going to fix the asteroid, and found himself in the strange position of wishing someone other than himself well.

"Biscuit?" offered Helen.

The Gnashersaurus took a step forwards.

"Not so fast, old boy!" came a rather posh but cruel voice.

Dennis, Gnasher and the Gnashersaurus turned to see Fletcher. Why was he suddenly so brave against the Gnashersaurus rex?

The Gnashersaurus growled.

Two other raptors stepped out of the jungle, and then Walter emerged behind them... on the back of a huge Spinosaurus!

"I don't believe you've met Mr Serious," Walter said bravely.

Mr Serious looked extremely serious. He was bigger than the Gnashersaurus, at 12 metres

long and seven metres high. His long crocodile-like mouth, full of long teeth, seemed to be extra long just to fit in some extra teeth.

Just to rub it in, this dinosaur also had proper arms. Not little raptor or T. rex arms, but big arms that ended in 30-centimetre claws. This Spinosaurus was more serious than Mum after a parents evening! (This Spinosaurus was actually the grandson of the Spinosaurus that attacked the school bus on Gran's school trip.)

It growled, its eyes fixed on them.

The Gnashersaurus let out a long, low growl in reply.

"Mate," Dennis said to him. "We don't need to do this."

The Gnashersaurus roared, and ran straight for Mr Serious.

The Spinosaurus ran forwards too, its jaws wide open. At the last moment, the Gnashersaurus ducked under Mr Serious's mouth and chomped his leg.

The thud of the impact knocked Walter off –

who, luckily for him, fell into a soft bush.

The raptors watched the epic battle, their eyes gleaming.

Walter looked away from the fight. His escape route was laid out for him. He had a clear run! The raptors weren't watching him anymore.

All this time he'd known that the only reason the raptors weren't eating him was because he was helping them with their Dennis problem. He was happy to help, but he knew that the second he stopped being useful he'd be dinner anyway. So he'd played along, acting brave, all the while knowing he was in a perilous situation.

The Spinosaurus brought his leg up, which lifted the Gnashersaurus's head up high enough for Mr Serious to bring his elbow down hard on the top of it.

The Gnashersaurus let go.

That was just showing off! The Gnashersaurus's puny little T. rex arms were so weedy that if he elbowed you on the noggin you'd hardly notice.

The Gnashersaurus staggered back.

Mr Serious glanced down at his injured leg. He'd had worse. He lunged forward, mouth open wide again.

The Gnashersaurus sidestepped, only just dodging his foe's jaws as Mr Serious scraped along his side.

The Spinosaurus went for Gnashy's tail instead, but Gnashy realised at the last moment and spun round as – SNAP! – Mr Serious's jaws snapped shut on fresh air.

I'm really glad I decided to write this extra bit after the end, aren't you? It's the best bit!

Gnashy chomped the Spinosaurus's bony sail. Mr Serious hardly felt it.

Walter was still watching from the bushes. A voice inside him was screaming RUN AWAY!, but he had to see what happened. Then Walter caught sight of one of the raptors looking at him. He'd stayed too long. Was it dinner time? He looked around for Dennis.

"Where's Dennis and that awful dog of his?" he shouted to the raptor.

The raptors realised Dennis and Gnasher were nowhere to be seen. They'd been too distracted by the awesome fight in front of them to notice their escape. They looked up the tiny mountain that had the asteroid on top.

Dennis and Gnasher were already halfway up!

Mr Serious chomped his jaws around Gnashy's right shoulder. The ferocity of the fight seemed to far outweigh the reason for it.

This was with good reason. Gnashersaurus and Mr Serious had history, going way back. Much like with Dennis and Walter, the reason their battle had started was lost in time. Mr Serious's memory was much, much better than the Gnashersaurus's but that didn't mean much. It was still pretty bad.

The raptors ran after Dennis and Gnasher.

Gnashy fell to the ground and rolled over, pulling the Spinosaurus onto him and flipping it onto its back. The Spinosaurus let go of Gnashy, twisted and rolled onto its side.

Near the top of the mini mountain, Dennis glanced back. He was missing the most epic dinosaur battle in history! He also noticed the raptors chasing after him, which was worrying – in the same way shark attacks are worrying.

Unfortunately, he'd now passed the cars that would have been easy to tip at them. Dennis was well inside where the park used to be.

Up ahead, though, there was a boat. A small row boat? Of course! It was one of the boats you could rent to go on the duck pond. It must have fallen as the mountain grew underneath it.

The boat had stuck on a root or vine. It was easy for Dennis to dislodge and send skidding down the steep slope towards the raptors. They dodged it easily, but doing so slowed them down and made them more cautious.

Next, Dennis came to one of the big fibreglass swan paddle boats you can also rent to go on the pond. So he sent that down too! Gradually the gap between Dennis and the raptors grew and grew.

YOU FLY IT THEN!

From his vantage point in the town hall, the Mayor was still watching through his telescope. Although Dennis had slowed the raptors down, he could see that Dennis might not get to the asteroid before the raptors got to him.

It was time for the Mayor to betray his son and help Dennis. Wilbur was fine with this. Walter had betrayed him in breaking the asteroid machine in the first place! And they were out of milk and biscuits.

"Helen," he said to Helen, "how are you at flying helicopters?"

"I, er... I'm only 15, sir," Helen told him. "This is just meant to be work experience. And it's the weekend. I shouldn't really be here!"

Wilbur looked crossly at the ceiling. "Can you fly a helicopter or not?"

"Yes, but—"

"Good! To the roof then!"

CHOMP! Gnashy chomped down onto the back of Mr Serious's neck.

Mr Serious tried to reach round and claw Gnashy but even his long, la-di-da show-off arms couldn't reach. So he stood up, throwing Gnashy off.

The Gnashersaurus fell on his back, and Mr Serious went for him.

Dennis and Gnasher reached the top and ran to the derelict "room" that housed the asteroid machine. Pipes and hoses littered the floor.

"How does all this go back together?" Dennis asked Gnasher.

Gnasher had no idea. All he knew was that, without some sort of plan, fixing this could take hours. Then he remembered something...

"GNASH! GNASH! GNASH!" he said, pointing his nose at Dennis's pocket. Dennis pulled out an old photo.

"I forgot I borrowed this photo off Gran

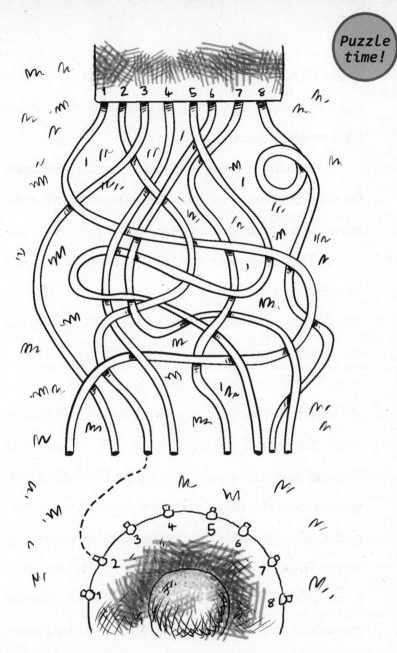

Can you connect all the hoses back to the machine in the correct order? One has been done for you.

earlier! Thanks Gnasher!" (See? I was right not to tell you before what Dennis borrowed from Gran. This was much cooler, wasn't it?)

Quickly, Dennis started jamming hoses back into the machine. He was too busy to notice the sound of an approaching helicopter.

The helicopter lurched and bucked like a bucking bronco, and sliced off the top of a palm. The Mayor, who was sitting in the back, nearly fell out of his seat.

"Who taught you how to fly?" he snapped at Helen.

Helen had had enough. "You fly it then!" she shouted over her shoulder. "I learned on a hingeless ultralight – this thing's fully articulated!"

"Fly smoothly, and none of your excuses or you're fired!" the Mayor shouted at Helen.

"GOOD!" Helen shouted back, and she shoved the throttle forwards, plunging the helicopter towards the ground.

The Mayor was faced with two harsh truths: one, it looked like Helen was going to crash the helicopter on purpose and, two, without Helen, he was going to have to go back to drinking Sandra's tea – and Sandra's tea was awful!

The Spinosaurus had one foot on Gnashy's tummy, holding him down. Mr Serious flexed his toes, digging his claws into Gnashy's soft underbelly.

He lowered his jaws, to chomp Gnashy's neck.

This was it! The Gnashersaurus was going to lose.

An Allosaurus slammed into the Spinosaurus's side, knocking him off balance.

Another Allosaurus ran into the fray. Minnie jumped off its back, and it too went for the Spinosaurus, slamming into its side.

Mr Serious was knocked over onto the ground.

"MINNIE TO THE RESCUE!" Minnie shouted.

Gnashy jumped up, ready to fight back...

A helicopter crashed into the fight arena. Well, not really crashed. It looked like it was going to crash, but at the absolute last moment, Helen pulled up and landed it so hard that the two ski-things underneath it snapped off.

Helen kicked her door open and, turning round once to shout, "Here you go. Sort this out!" to the Mayor, stormed off.

A Majungasaurus burst forth out of the bushes. These dinosaurs are similar in shape to a T. rex only half the size, but with a somehow meaner look.

"GRRRRRAAAAAAHHHHH!"

it growled at Helen.

Helen gave it a stern look and shouted, "Back off, buster. I've had a bad day!"

The Majungasaurus had piled on the pounds recently. It decided it should probably miss lunch, this one time.

The Mayor staggered out of the damaged helicopter, looked at the four-way dinosaur rumble, and put his hands on his hips in his best "I'm in charge" pose.

"Now look here!" he shouted.

CHOMP!

The Spinosaurus ate him!

I know, right? It's a bit shocking. This is meant to be a kids' book. But Mr Serious ate Wilbur – I can't do anything about that.

The Spinosaurus spat him out.

"Urrrrrgh!" Mr Serious said, wiping his tongue with his claws. The Mayor obviously tasted horrible!

Wilbur screamed. He was covered from head to toe in thick dinosaur saliva, and it seemed like Mr Serious was just getting over a heavy cold, judging by all the green.

"Doesn't anyone have any respect for the office of Mayor?" He coughed and spluttered. "Helen, do you have a tissue?" he asked.

But Helen was long gone.

By this time, the raptors had reached Dennis and Gnasher. Fletcher was just about to say something witty and posh but also a bit scary, when Dennis plugged in the last hose.

The machine holding the asteroid together

burst into life, and the two halves clamped shut.

SHOOMP! Suddenly the asteroid disappeared. In fact, it hadn't disappeared, but it was now tiny, the size of a pea. Its own incredible weight (or gravity) had squashed it down tiny.

It had worked! Dennis had mended the asteroid!

Fletcher gave Dennis a stern look, and the raptors all ran for Dennis and Gnasher... and SHOOMP! SHOOMP! SHOOMP! they all shrank as the effect spread.

But when you shrink, you don't feel like you're shrinking. From your point of view, everything around you gets suddenly huge. So Fletcher found himself running towards an enormous Gnasher! He slammed on the brakes as Gnasher gnashed at him, turned and quickly ran away.

The ground under Dennis shook and quaked. The mountain began to shrink. Dennis and Gnasher fell over.

Everything from the island seemed to be shrinking first, starting with the bits which were closest to the asteroid.

Mr Serious turned to Gnashy. He was ready to restart the fight, even if Gnashy did have extra back-up from Minnie's Allosauruses. But because he was nearer the asteroid, suddenly – SHOOMP! – Mr Serious was tiny.

I asked a scientist how and why what happened next happened. She didn't really know. Her best guess was that everything from the island was used to being squashed down small. Their atoms and molecules had always been squashed together, so they were the creatures and objects most easily re-squashed.

All across town, trees and bushes and dinosaurs and old steam trains and roots and vines – everything from the island – began to shrink.

SHOOMP! SHOOMP! SHOOMP!

The carpet of jungle under them was pulling

everything back to Duck Island. The tumbling pre-historic jungle-flood happened in reverse. And anything on its feet was pulled off its feet.

Over at Dennis's house, Dad was holding Bea as he looked out of the living room window.

"Bye-bye, dinosaurs!" he said sadly as he took Bea's hand to make it wave goodbye. "Can you say 'Bye-bye, dinosaurs'?"

"Byed-byed, dinnerslobs!" Bea said.

"Clever girl!" said Dad.

OLD BEAN

Eventually it ended, and everything was back the way it had been before this all happened.

At some point in the confusion, Dennis and Gnasher had been shrunk too. It was hard not to be when you were so close to the asteroid. They were halfway up the mini mountain, on the ground near Fletcher, when it happened. Gnasher gave Dennis his best "Uh-oh" look – again.

Fletcher stood up. He looked about. His friends didn't seem to be around. He smiled at Dennis. "This was a fun little game, old bean," Fletcher said. "We'll have to play again sometime."

And with that, he zipped off down the mountain into the jungle and was gone.

"That was weird!" said Dennis to himself. He thought a lot about that moment afterwards. Why had Fletcher left him, when he could have attacked?

Dennis couldn't be sure, but there had seemed to be something close to respect for Dennis in Fletcher's eye.

Dennis was battered and bruised, scuffed and scraped. He was muddy and he smelled bad, but he had sort of enjoyed the whole experience. Well, it wasn't fun at the time, but he enjoyed remembering everything.

Perhaps Fletcher had enjoyed it too, the deadly game.

"What do you fancy doing now?" Minnie

asked. Dennis turned round. Minnie was standing there, hardly a scratch on her, looking ready to do it all again.

"After I get off this island, I want a lie down!"

Gnasher gave Dennis his best "Oh yes! A lie down would be awesome" look.

"Lightweights!" Minnie teased.

The three of them stumbled down to the bottom of the mountain together.

"What about the shrinky do-hicky?" Minnie asked. "What's to stop anyone turning it off again?"

"Urrrgh! I dunno," Dennis groaned. "Can that be someone else's job?"

Nearby, the Mayor staggered out of some bushes. "I'll sort that," he said. "I'll have so much concrete poured over that thing, it'll never come apart again!"

CLUMPH!

Walter fell out of a nearby tree. He struggled to his feet.

"This isn't over, Dennis!" he said, "I'll—"

"I'll give you 20 pounds if you don't fight or betray me for the rest of the day," his father interrupted.

Walter thought about it for a moment then said, "Okay."

"Do you want an ice cream?" Minnie asked.

This seemed a bit of an odd, sideways jump

in conversation. They all looked at her.

"The ice cream van's just there," she said, pointing ahead.

Sure enough, there was Mr Icy in the middle of the jungle. Inside was a rather dazed and confused looking ice cream man.

As the Mayor bought the kids ice creams, he said, "My first plan for this island was to turn it into a park. My second plan was to let hunters hunt here. But my third plan is to leave it alone and act like it doesn't exist!"

For the first and possibly last time, Dennis agreed with him.

THE END...

"What do you mean, 'the end'?" asked Mr Icy. What about me? I'm on a dinosaur island?! What happens to me?!"

Well, I'm not saying there wasn't quite a bit of tidying up to do. The shrink-back was far from perfect. An ice cream man, a hairdresser, a window cleaner, a cartoonist for a popular weekly children's comic, and several other people had ended up on the island, and quite a few dinosaurs were left hanging around in Beanotown. So it was a few weeks before everything was back to normal, but I'm not writing all that. Who wants to read about weeks of tidying up?!

"GNASH!"

Everyone turned. The Gnashersaurus was on top of the mini mountain, doing his best roaring and gnashing and his best "Look at me! I'm the king of the castle"-ing.

"The end," said Dennis, as he sat back in his chair at the coffee shop. "Is that a good enough story?" he asked me.

"Yeah," I said.

I couldn't take my eyes off the hipster who looked like a Viking behind the counter. He was obviously a Viking trying to look like a hipster!

"Yeah, that'll do."

"Worth a hot chocolate for me and a cappuccino for my friend?" Dennis asked, gesturing to the elephant, or "French spy", depending on who you believe.

I had to agree.

As I placed their drinks on the table, I said to myself, "This story should keep the wolf from the door, for a while at least." I was of course referring to the wolf my publisher had a habit of setting on writers who didn't write enough.

The elephant slurped up some coffee as I sat down, and blasted it out of his trunk into my face in distaste.

"Mate! You didn't forget the sugar, did you?" Dennis asked.

THE ACTUAL, PROPER END.

Or is it?